THE VALE VINEYARD KILLER

An enthralling murder mystery with a twist

FRANCES LLOYD

Detective Inspector Jack Dawes Mystery Book 8

JOFFE BOOKS

Joffe Books, London
www.joffebooks.com

First published in Great Britain in 2021

Cover art by Dee Dee Book Covers

ISBN: 978-1-78931-960-6

PROLOGUE

Richington Vale Winery — twenty years ago

In the bedroom of a vine worker's cottage, Thomas Baker lay dying. His wife, Linda, sat at his bedside, holding his hand and weeping quietly, for fear of alarming the children. With an intuition beyond her years, ten-year-old Samantha was pretty sure she knew what was about to happen. What she couldn't foresee was the perilous journey her life would take as a result of her father's death. She reached out for her little brother's hand. Michael looked up at her, frightened eyes filled with tears. At just seven, he didn't quite understand why his father was ill, but he cried because his mother was crying.

Initially, Baker had been suffering from headaches, blurred vision and dizziness. He had ignored it, dismissing it as fatigue. It was late November and the pruning season had been well underway. As an experienced worker, he made more than thirty cuts per minute, many hours a day, for many weeks. It was a good earner. But as the weeks had progressed, his symptoms had worsened. He had begun wheezing, his chest had tightened, he had developed a persistent cough that had affected his pruning speed and consequently

1

his earnings. Then had come the abdominal cramps, the diarrhoea and nausea. Reluctantly, he had taken to his bed and Linda had called the doctor.

Dr Anstruther was employed by the Richington Vale Winery to look after the health of the employees and their families. Over the years, he had dealt with virtually every accident, mishap and illness that could befall viticulture workers. After several visits to the Bakers' cottage, he finally conceded that there was nothing more he could do.

'I'm sorry, Linda. Thomas has only a few days at most.'

She was devastated. 'But he's only forty-three. I don't understand. He used to be so fit and strong. How could this have happened, Doctor?'

Anstruther picked up a packet of cigarettes from the bedside table. 'How long has Thomas been smoking these?'

'All the time I've known him. That's at least twenty years. I believe he started smoking when he was still at school. He's never without a cigarette in his mouth. Says it helps him to concentrate. I used to joke that he only took it out at mealtimes, to eat.'

The doctor shrugged. 'Well, there's your answer. Eventually, the poison catches up with you.' He held the packet in front of Samantha and Michael. 'Understand this, children. Smoking affects every aspect of your health. Leave it alone.'

* * *

The death certificate recorded that Thomas Baker had died from respiratory failure resulting from pulmonary oedema and nicotine poisoning. As if losing her husband wasn't enough, Linda discovered there was even worse to come. It seemed the terms of the tied cottage ended with the death of the worker. There was apparently no way around it. Not only was she without a husband, but she had to leave the home they had lived in since they were married. It seemed there was no company pension, death benefit or life insurance.

'Where's Daddy?' Michael couldn't understand the concept of death no matter how many times Linda tried to explain.

'Daddy's gone to heaven, Mikey. He's with the angels. Do you remember the vicar explaining it to you at Daddy's funeral?'

'That's rubbish!' Samantha snapped. 'There's no such place as heaven. There's no God, either. If there were, why would he have let Dad die?' Samantha had ceased to believe all the stories about God loving every living thing after her cat got run over. She certainly wasn't swallowing any of that nonsense about Dad leaving them to go and sit on a cloud and play a harp, like the picture Miss Chambers had shown her at school.

Linda reprimanded her. 'Sam, don't upset your brother. We must all stay strong, especially now that we have to move away.'

They had little money and no home. Her only option was to take the children to live with her parents in the north. They were elderly and not in the best of health. Linda hoped she might be entitled to some sort of widow's benefit. Failing that, she planned to find a job. She had no idea what. At forty and with no qualifications, it would be hard. Her flaming auburn hair, which Thomas had so loved, was turning prematurely white with the worry. It was a desperate situation but she had little choice. The owners of the winery had given her the small amount of sick pay due to Thomas at the time of his death. As they pointed out, they were not obliged to pay anything more, as he had died due to his unhealthy lifestyle. She had wondered whether she should consult solicitors, but that would be expensive and she needed every penny to support the children until she got back on her feet.

CHAPTER ONE

Wine brings to light the hidden secrets of the soul.
Quintus Horatius Flaccus (Horace, 65–8 BCE)

The present

It was a hot summer's day in the Richington Vale vineyards. Flowering was coming to an end and the fruit set was beginning, the critical stage when the flowers turn to grapes. At this time of year, the guided tours were popular. On that particular day, a dozen or so visitors were admiring the stunning views through the wide picture window in the tasting room. Row upon row of Chardonnay grapevines stretched down the hill and far into the distance. The sky was turquoise, the vines green and lush. But despite the undeniable beauty of its surroundings, visitors would have been wrong to assume the winery was built on harmonious benevolence and goodwill. The Richington-Blythe family, owners of the estate since 1953, had their sights set firmly on giving French winemakers serious competition. And to this end, they were tenacious, ruthless and without conscience.

* * *

Bob Beacham had been employed by the Richington-Blythes for nearly thirty years. He had worked his way up from general dogsbody to vineyard manager, so there was little he didn't know about turning grapes into superlative wine. That afternoon, he was checking the fermentation in the huge storage tanks. It was a long and arduous job, working alone in the vast, underground chamber, but it was important. He moved along the line of tanks, climbing each ladder, lifting the hatch to look inside, then chalking the details on the blackboards fixed to the front. Working up a thirst, he wondered how long it would be before Wendy brought his mug of tea from the canteen.

He heard the heavy, reinforced door open behind him. Good, he was parched. Maybe there'd be a biscuit to go with it. He called out, 'Thanks, love.' After a few moments, when she didn't answer, he turned around to see why.

It wasn't Wendy. He called to the figure in the visitor's white coat and hat, wondering how he'd got past the keypad entry system. It mustn't have reset after he'd closed the door. He'd need to report that to security, or anyone could walk in.

'The guided tour isn't due down here for another half an hour, mate. Did you get lost?'

The intruder came closer, and he recognized him. 'What are you doing in here?'

There was no answer, but an unexpected shove caught him off balance. 'Oi! Pack it in! What's the matter with you?'

There was another hefty push and Beacham swung a punch in defence, but missed. Another assault sent him staggering backwards. He fell heavily and his head made contact with the closing valve of the nearest tank. The impact knocked him cold.

His assailant hoisted the unconscious man in a fireman's lift and carried him up the tank's ladder. It took just seconds to heave open the hatch and wedge Beacham's head and shoulders inside. Calmly, the attacker climbed back down the ladder, pushed his way out through the main door and made sure that the red security light re-engaged. Then he climbed up the stone steps, discarded his polyurethane gloves in a nearby bin, and strolled towards the exit.

* * *

Discreet alcoves in the state-of-the-art tasting room displayed elegantly placed bottles of Richington Vale wine, bearing the distinctive gold label. Sébastien Richington-Blythe, the tour guide, held his flute of pale gold liquid aloft, so that the sunlight glinted off the bubbles. 'This sparkling wine that you're tasting, ladies and gentlemen, will give the winemakers of Champagne a run for their money. Note the fine bead and nutty finish.'

There was a collective hum of approval and noisy slurping. A few of them understood what they were tasting; others were there because it was on their holiday itinerary and they'd already paid for the excursion. The rest were just glad of a cold drink on a hot day.

'Richington Vale is one of the oldest family-owned vineyards in England.' Sébastien went round topping up glasses. 'It was founded in 1953 by my grandfather, Air Commodore Sir Donald Richington-Blythe, DFC — known affectionately as "Ducky" to his RAF pals. His lifelong love affair with wine began as a young pilot in the Second World War, when he crashed his Lancaster near a vineyard in Bordeaux. Friendly French farmworkers gave him shelter and shared their precious wine with him. On returning to his family estate in Richington Vale, he declared that he loved wine "so bloody much" that he was going to dedicate the land attached to the Richington-Blythe country manor to growing the stuff.' Sébastien proudly pointed to the Gold Medal label on the bottle. 'Following grandfather's success in producing fine wine, my father, Jolyon Richington-Blythe, took over the business in 1989, bought more acres of the surrounding countryside, expanded the vineyards and gave employment to many local workers. This, ladies and gentlemen, was the start of the proud heritage which has been the foundation of the Richington Vale brand ever since. We now boast an events suite, for corporate seminars, conferences and incentive programmes, complete with quality catering, provided by Coriander's Cuisine, a superb local company. For those of you interested in learning more about wine, a comprehensive tasting course is run by Suzy Black, our resident Master of Wine. If anyone is planning an event, please let my sister, Marianne, know and she will be happy to organize the entire experience for you.' He set down his glass. 'Let's move on now to the storage tanks.'

Clad in their white coats and hats, they trooped down a flight of stone steps to a heavily reinforced door. Sébastien keyed in the code and pulled it open. Inside the vast underground chamber, they gazed up at row upon row of massive stainless-steel tanks. They stood on sturdy steel legs on a two-foot concrete plinth.

'These giants are capable of holding over five hundred gallons of wine. They contain the whole of last year's precious vintage. The process involves . . .'

Sébastien had scarcely started to explain when a chippy lad at the back interrupted. 'What's he doing?' He pointed to the tank at the far end of the chamber, where they could see a man with his head and shoulders inside the open hatch.

Sébastien looked. 'That's Bob, one of our more experienced workers and the vineyard manager. He's been with us nearly thirty years. Right now, he's monitoring the volume and fermentation of the wine.'

'Is he all right?' asked a concerned lady. 'He doesn't seem to be moving.'

'I'm sure he's absolutely fine,' replied Sébastien, who wasn't sure at all. 'We pride ourselves on the highest level of health and safety at Richington Vale.' He spoke urgently into the intercom clipped to his shoulder. 'Robbie, this is Seb. Could you send a couple of colleagues down into the storage chamber? Right away, please. I think Bob could use some help, and I'm busy with a tour at the moment.'

Minutes later, a couple of men in overalls bearing the Richington Vale logo hurried down the steps and through the fortified door. One of them climbed up the ladder where Bob was still not moving. Almost immediately, he stumbled back down. 'Mr Sébastien, I think you need to see this.'

* * *

The tourists were hastily escorted back to reception, where Marianne issued replacement tickets with profuse apologies for the disruption of the tour. 'I'm so sorry your visit had to be cut short, ladies and gentlemen, but I do hope you'll come back and finish the tour. Please accept a bottle of Richington Vale's Gold Medal Chardonnay with the compliments of the management. Passes can be handed back to Wendy on the desk, and she will sign you out.'

One or two of the more curious would have preferred to stay to find out what had happened. Things had livened up — it was the most interesting part of the tour. As they were climbing back on the coach, they heard sirens and an ambulance. A police car drew up outside the winery.

'I wonder what that was all about,' said the chippy lad. 'Why do coppers always say, "Move along — nothing to see here," when there obviously is something to see?'

'I reckon that bloke was stuck,' resolved his girlfriend. 'D'you s'pose he'll be OK?'

'Nah. I watched him and he never moved once, not even his hands. I mean, if your head was stuck inside a hatch, you'd be pushing like mad with your hands to get it out, wouldn't you? You wouldn't let them hang down by your sides, like he did. I reckon he's carked it.'

* * *

And after the paramedics had examined him, they confirmed that Bob had indeed 'carked it', if not precisely in those words. Sergeant Norman Parsloe and a couple of uniformed constables from the Kings Richington Police supervised the removal of the unfortunate man from the hatch of the storage tank. Jolyon and Sébastien watched anxiously.

'I don't understand it,' said Jolyon. 'Our safety record is second to none. What could have gone wrong?'

'It's just a terrible accident, Father.' Sébastien had already decided. 'It looks like Bob climbed up to see how the fermentation was progressing, leaned in too far and somehow got stuck.'

Sergeant Parsloe was making notes in his book. 'You mean the poor devil drowned in wine?'

'No, not at all. There's a gap between the surface of the wine and the top of the tank. But there's very little oxygen, due to the biological activity of the fermentation. I'm afraid Bob would have lost consciousness very quickly.'

'Probably followed by cardiac arrest,' added one of the paramedics, helpfully.

Parsloe snapped his notebook shut. 'This will have to be reported, sir. The HSE will want to get involved, never mind the coroner.'

'Yes, of course, officer.' Jolyon nodded. 'We'll make sure all the correct procedures are followed. But I can assure you, the process is perfectly safe, as long as the operative follows the specified instructions.'

The paramedics were placing the dead man on a stretcher when Parsloe spotted something. 'Wait a minute. Can you turn him over, please?'

They rolled the body over and Parsloe pointed to a blood-soaked wound, matting the hair on the dead man's head. 'How did he come to injure the back of his head, if he was leaning forward?'

Jolyon and Sébastien looked at each other, guardedly. 'I've no idea, officer. Maybe he did it before he climbed up the ladder,' offered Sébastien.

'I don't think so, sir. A blow like that would have knocked him out.'

'Perhaps the cover of the hatch fell on him,' Jolyon suggested.

They looked up at the still upright cover. 'It wasn't down on his head when we pulled him out, Sarge,' recalled the constable.

Parsloe gestured to the paramedics. 'Leave the body where it is, please.' Then to Constable Johnson, 'Cordon off the area. I'm treating this as a suspicious death and this is now a crime scene.'

Both Sébastien and his father protested. 'Is this really necessary, officer? Surely it's something we can handle in-house. A sad but unfortunate accident.'

Jolyon was rather more forthright. 'A police investigation will delay production. We can't afford any bad publicity. Can't we come to some arrangement, Sergeant?'

Parsloe scowled. 'I hope you don't mean what I think you mean, sir.' He turned away and radioed the station. 'This is Sergeant Parsloe. I need to speak to Inspector Jack Dawes of the Murder Investigation Team.'

CHAPTER TWO

It was Detective Sergeant Michael 'Bugsy' Malone who took Sergeant Parsloe's call. DI Dawes was in Chief Superintendent Garwood's office, discussing the clear-up rate, or rather the lack of it. Garwood always blamed any shortfall in performance on Dawes, whether the inspector had been accountable or not. The alternative was that he'd have to take responsibility himself, and that would never do. Garwood was ambitious with hopes of retiring as chief constable, maybe even with a knighthood. He couldn't afford any slip-ups at this stage in his career. If he detected anything brown and unpleasant heading in the direction of a fan, Garwood was the first to duck. His wife, Cynthia, was an old school friend of Jack's wife, Corrie Dawes. Together, the ladies had contrived to interfere in several MIT cases in an effort to 'assist', frequently getting themselves into all manner of scrapes. It hadn't deterred them.

When his phone rang, Bugsy had just taken a huge bite out of a warm doughnut from the canteen. He spoke through sticky lips, coated in jam and sugar. 'Hello, Norman. What can we do for you?'

'I need some help, Bugsy.'

'It's not your grumbling hernia playing up again, is it? Try loosening your Y-fronts.'

'No, it's nothing to do with that. I'm at the reception desk of the Richington Vale Winery.'

'All right for some,' quipped Bugsy. 'No danger of some free samples, I suppose?'

'No, but I've got a body for you.'

'I'd rather have a bottle of wine, if it's all the same to you.' He took another bite of doughnut.

'I'm serious. Uniform was called out to what was reported as a fatal accident. Bloke got jammed in the top of a wine storage tank. But when we got him down and the ambulance lads turned him over, he had a blooming great gash on the back of his head. Looks suspicious to me.'

Bugsy swallowed the last of his doughnut. 'OK, Norman. We're on our way.'

* * *

'What do you know about this winery, Bugsy?'

Dawes and Malone were in the car, speeding towards the vineyard and hoping the public hadn't been trampling all over the scene.

'Only that it's been in the Richington-Blythe family since World War Two. They own most of Richington Vale, including the pub. It's called the Blythe Spirit.'

'Very whimsical,' said Jack. 'Any trouble in the village?'

'Not trouble, exactly. I remember Uniform being called out to break up a fight, outside in the pub car park. Just the usual drunken brawl that got out of hand. A few bones were broken and the vicar skinned his knuckles, but it wasn't serious. No beer was spilled.'

The village of Richington Vale was situated some five miles from the market town of Kings Richington. It was quintessentially English. Pretty thatched cottages, built using honey-coloured stone from the ruined eleventh-century Richington Abbey, were clustered around the village green. The River Richington, a minor tributary of the Thames, chuckled gently through the village between the main street and a water meadow, and was home to paddling ducks, gliding swans and nervous trout. Good old-fashioned shops lined the narrow streets, including a butcher, a grocer, a baker and a florist. The cosy pub was the centre of village life and the community social hub. Opposite, a tiny post office served as a corner shop and tea room.

Most of the villagers living in the cottages worked for the winery in some capacity, as had their fathers and mothers before them. In times of economic hardship, the Spirit of the Grapes was said to come down from the vineyard above the village and leave food at the homes of the poor. This custom had died out with the advent of the current generation of Richington-Blythes.

Bugsy pointed to an elaborate billboard on the roadside ahead.

WELCOME TO RICHINGTON VALE WINERY
A FAMILY-RUN VINEYARD SINCE 1953
THE HOME OF AWARD-WINNING WINES
'There it is, guv. Turn right, here.'

* * *

Down in the winery storage chamber, Forensics had already arrived and were busy examining the crime scene — if, indeed, it was a crime scene. The pathologist was kneeling beside the corpse, taking samples from the head wound with tweezers. His assistant, Miss Catwater, was placing them carefully in sterilized pots. The doctor looked up as the police officers approached. 'Hey, guys, would you mind not standing so close. You're in my light. Who the hell are you, anyway?' He had a thin, reedy voice.

'Doctor, this is DI Dawes and DS Malone from the Murder Investigation Team,' Marigold Catwater explained.

The doctor clambered to his feet. He was tall and lean, with alarming orange hair sprouting from beneath the hood of his protective suit. The virtually chinless face was liberally peppered with freckles. 'How do you do?' He went to shake hands then realized he was wearing surgical gloves, so nodded vaguely instead.

'Where's Big Ron?' blurted Bugsy, without thinking. 'Big Ron' was the affectionate nickname they had for Dr Veronica Hardacre, the usual pathologist. She was not only big in stature but had a superb scientific brain. She also sported bristling black eyebrows and a matching moustache. Big Ron took no prisoners, and senior police officers asked 'damn fool' questions at their peril.

'Doctor Hardacre is on holiday,' replied Miss Catwater primly. 'This is Doctor Gavin Golightly. He's acting as locum.'

'Blimey!' exclaimed Bugsy. He was trying to imagine Big Ron walking along Blackpool seafront, eating an ice cream. Or even more unlikely, lying on the beach in her bikini. 'Has she gone somewhere nice?'

'Game fishing in Bermuda,' replied Miss Catwater. 'She emailed me a video of herself, strapped into the fighting chair on a yacht. She was wrestling a giant marlin.'

'Did she win?' asked Bugsy, impressed.

'Of course,' replied Marigold.

'Fascinating though this is,' observed Dawes, 'we should really like to know how this man died, Doctor Golightly.'

He frowned. 'So would I, Inspector. So would I.' He knelt down again and peered into the dead man's soulless eyes, as if seeking some hypnotic transfer of evidence.

Jack and Bugsy exchanged glances. 'Do we know who he is?' ventured Jack.

Golightly shrugged. 'Not a clue.'

A nearby SOCO was dusting for fingerprints. 'His name's Bob Beacham, sir. He was the vineyard manager. He's worked here for thirty years, according to the owners. They couldn't understand how the accident could have happened. Apparently, he's very experienced.'

'Was it an accident, Doc?' asked Bugsy.

The pathologist shrugged again. 'Might have been. Can't be sure until after I've got him on the slab and pulled him apart. Even then, I shouldn't bet next month's salary on it.' He nodded to the waiting mortuary attendants. 'You can take him away now, if you like.' He packed his instrument bag, gave Jack and Bugsy a tepid smile and strode off. Miss Catwater rolled her eyes and trotted after him.

Bugsy watched him depart. 'D'you suppose he's in the right job, guv?'

'Well, he doesn't fill me with confidence, but give him a chance. Not all pathologists are up to Doctor Hardacre's standard. Doesn't mean he won't find something useful, given time.'

'I won't hold me breath,' muttered Bugsy.

Dawes and Malone made their way back to reception where Sergeant Parsloe was questioning Marianne. He looked relieved to see them. 'Oh good, you're here, Jack. This is Miss Marianne Richington-Blythe. She's the daughter of the vineyard owner.' Then to her, 'These officers need to have a word with your father.'

Marianne was olive-skinned with glossy dark hair, tied back in a ponytail. Jack estimated she was about thirty, possibly a little older.

'Please, follow me, gentlemen. We'll go up to the house. My father and brother will be there.' She had an attractive Mediterranean accent, possibly Bordeaux French.

The house was spectacular — four storeys, each with stunning views over the verdant vineyards. It had been deliberately designed to be stately, rather than to harmonize with the landscape. It even boasted a flagpole on the roof, the flag bearing the coat of arms of the Richington-Blythes. Designed by the air commodore himself, it was a pastiche of grapes, aircraft and wine bottles. It looked much like the debris left behind in the officers' mess after Dining-In Night.

Marianne showed them into an opulent drawing room. The décor was vintage, French-inspired with heavy brocade curtains and matching upholstery. A pair of art deco cameo glass vases containing extravagant bunches of professionally arranged flowers stood either side of the magnificent fireplace. Jolyon and Sébastien were tasting wine from several bottles in an antique château-style wine cabinet.

'Papa, this is Inspector Dawes and Sergeant Malone. They want to speak to you about Beacham.'

Jolyon glanced briefly at the badge that Dawes held out. 'It's a nasty business, Inspector, but accidents do happen in the best regulated of vineyards. In my experience, it's nearly always due to employees not following health and safety regulations. I'm not sure how you think we can help.' He held out a glass of wine. 'Can I tempt you? This is one of our best vintages.'

Jack shook his head. 'No, thank you, sir. You seem very sure that it was an accident.'

'What else could it have been?' Sébastien's tone was defensive. 'You surely don't suspect some bizarre suicide? Beacham was a happily married man with grown-up children.'

'We don't suspect anything yet, sir,' said Malone. 'It's early days. We'll be following all lines of enquiry once we get the post-mortem report.'

'Is a post-mortem absolutely necessary?' drawled Jolyon. 'We know how the poor man died. He leaned too far into the tank, became stuck and suffocated through lack of oxygen. A post-mortem would be a waste of public money, surely?'

'What about the injury to the back of his head?' asked Jack. 'The coroner will want that explained to his satisfaction before reaching a verdict.'

'Did your forensic people find any kind of weapon that might have been used to inflict the injury?' Seb was pouring himself another glass of sparkling Chardonnay. He didn't wait for an answer. 'No, I thought not. Bob obviously had some kind of fall, banged his head but continued with his duties, despite suffering debilitating concussion.'

'So there you have it, officers. No mystery, just very unfortunate.' Jolyon nodded to Marianne. 'If there's nothing more, my daughter will show you out.'

Jack wasn't about to be rushed. 'We'll need details of the deceased's work patterns and also his address, so that officers can notify his widow and appoint a family liaison officer, if required.'

'No need for that, Inspector. Naturally, I've already sent a member of staff to break the sad news. Marianne handles all the HR business. She'll provide you with any other information you need.' He dismissed them with a wave. 'Goodbye.'

Marianne Richington-Blythe was either unable or unwilling to provide anything more than they already knew. Her partner, Robbie, hovered menacingly in the background while she brought up the records they needed on her computer. They thanked her for her help and left.

They had almost reached the car, when a plump, middle-aged lady in a white overall and protective hairnet came running after them. By the time she caught up, she was puffed out. 'Officers?' She stopped to catch her breath. 'You are the police officers here about poor Bob's death, aren't you?'

'Well, if we aren't, there's a couple of blokes going around who look exactly like us.' Bugsy's obscure humour was lost on some folk, and she was one of them. She looked puzzled.

'Yes, we are,' said Jack. 'How can we help Mrs . . .?'

'Wendy. I work in the canteen and I help Miss Marianne with some of the routine paperwork on the desk. The thing is, I saw him.'

'Saw who, love?' asked Bugsy, patiently.

'The man who murdered Bob.'

'Who said he was murdered, Wendy?' Jack was interested now.

'Well, what else could it have been? Bob has worked here longer than I have, and that's over thirty years. There's no way he would have had a careless accident, like management are trying to make out. It's my belief he was bashed over the head and then he was murdered. And I saw who did it.'

News obviously travelled fast, especially bad news. They put her in the back of the car, while Bugsy wrote what she said in his notebook.

'It was all my fault, really. If I'd been on time with Bob's tea, I might have been able to prevent it, but the urn was playing up, so by the time I'd fixed it, poured out the tea, got a plate of biscuits and taken them over to the storage chamber, there were police cars everywhere and poor Bob was dead.'

'Who did you see, Wendy?' Jack thought this was probably a waste of time but when you hadn't any clues, you couldn't afford to dismiss anything.

'I saw a man wearing a visitor's white coat and hat walking away from the storage chamber towards the exit. It was while I was in the canteen, trying to get the urn to work. You have a clear view of the entry and exit from there.'

'Did you recognize him at all?' asked Bugsy, more in hope than expectation.

'No, dear. I only saw him from the back. But they're not allowed to wander about on their own, for health and safety reasons, so I assumed he'd just got fed up and was looking for the coach. It was only later on that I realized he wasn't with the tour party at all. You see, I sign them in, hand out their passes, then take them back when they leave. Today, I signed them all in, then I signed them all out again, after the tour was aborted — and there weren't any passes missing.'

'He could have given his pass to someone else to hand in,' suggested Bugsy.

'He could have, dear, but he didn't. It was one person, one pass. I counted them.'

Jack had a sudden thought. 'If he wasn't on the tour, how did he get hold of the white coat and hat?'

'Didn't you notice when you came in? There are lots of them, hanging up in the entrance porch. He could just walk in and help himself. But what I don't understand is how he got into the storage tank room in the first place. There's a keypad on the door and you have to know the code. Bob wouldn't have let a stranger in.'

'So what you're saying is that it was an inside job — someone who knew the code.'

'All I'm saying is that I know he wasn't on that tour because of the colour of his hair. I could see it, below his hat at the back.'

'What does the colour of his hair have to do with anything?' Bugsy was getting confused.

'It was ginger. Nobody on the tour today had ginger hair.'

* * *

'What did you make of that, guv?' asked Bugsy, on the way back to the station.

Jack pursed his lips. 'When we were called in, I reckoned it would turn out to be an industrial accident — nothing suspicious, just Norman being extra cautious. Now I'm pretty sure, like Wendy, that there's much more to it.'

'D'you reckon she's a reliable witness?'

'Yes. Ladies like her are as sharp as tacks. It's just a pity she didn't see chummy's face, so we could get an e-fit. It's perfectly possible he could have pinched a white coat and hat then blended in with the visitors, so we don't even have a description of the clothes he was wearing. The ginger hair could be useful, though.'

'If he knew the security code, and he obviously did, he must be a member of staff,' said Bugsy.

Jack was pensive. 'Not necessarily. Maybe he knew someone who works there and they told him.'

'Why would they do that, guv?'

'That's what we need to find out.'

'Cagey lot, weren't they, the Richington-Blythes?' recalled Bugsy. 'Very anxious to fob us off.'

'Very quick off the mark to get to the widow before we did, too. Hopefully, the post-mortem will tell us more.'

'Yeah — right.' Bugsy was unconvinced.

CHAPTER THREE

Next morning, DS Malone and DC Aled Williams arrived at the mortuary to see what, if anything, the post-mortem had revealed. DI Dawes only attended if it was essential. The smells and cloying atmosphere of the cold, white-tiled examination room always stuck in his throat and made him nauseous.

When Dr Hardacre conducted a post-mortem, she liked to have music playing quietly in the background. More often than not, it was a Chopin nocturne or Schubert's *Trout Quintet*. She believed soothing music was respectful to the departed and compensated in some way for the indignities she was obliged to inflict. Not so, Gavin Golightly. As they pushed open the doors, they were hit by a wall of sound.

'*Duw!*' exclaimed Aled, taking a step back.

'Bloody hell!' Bugsy reckoned the last time he'd heard a racket like that was when the shelves he'd put up in the kitchen gave way, and all his wife's pots and pans slid off onto the tiled floor. That was the trouble with do-it-yourself — very often, it did it back. 'What's that 'orrible noise? It's enough to loosen your fillings.'

'It's heavy metal, Sarge,' bellowed Aled above the distorted guitars and vigorous vocals. 'I don't recognize the band, though.'

'You call that a band?' Bugsy shouted back. In his view, a band was when they all played the same tune.

Miss Catwater, implacable as ever, stood holding a dish to collect any bits and pieces the doctor saw fit to remove. Bugsy wondered why she wasn't similarly deafened. Then he saw the earplugs.

Dr Golightly turned down the clamour, so they could hold a conversation. 'It's my band, Sergeant Malone. We formed it at medical school and we've been playing together ever since. We call ourselves Necrotic Nightmare.'

'Got any gigs coming up?' Aled was trying to picture him on stage, screaming into a mike and shaking his orange hair about. He could see quite a lot of it, scrunched into a man-bun, under the doctor's cap.

'Oh yes. We have one on Saturday in the Richington Community Centre. I'll get you tickets, if you'd like to come.'

'Thanks all the same, Doc, but it's my night to put the bins out.' Malone peered at the body on the examination table. 'What can you tell us about this poor sod?'

Dr Golightly looked mildly surprised at the question. 'He sustained a blow on the head, then he suffocated from lack of oxygen.'

Malone fought hard to suppress a remark about a 'blinding glimpse of the bleeding obvious'. Instead, he asked, 'Er . . . how do you think he got the clout on the head, Doc?'

'He could have fallen down, I suppose, or someone might have hit him with something.' He went to turn the heavy metal up again, but Malone put his bulk between him and the device.

'Any idea what that something might have been?'

Golightly felt for his sunken chin and, having found it, rubbed it, thoughtfully. 'A rock, possibly, or a lump hammer.'

'Did the SOCOs find anything like that near the scene?' asked Aled.

'If they did, they didn't tell me.'

'Does the shape of the wound give us any clues to a possible weapon?' Aled was trying to think what Dr Hardacre would look for.

Golightly had another squint at the cadaver's crown. 'It might be grooved. Difficult to see a shape, with his hair stuck to it like that. A flat object — metal maybe. Or it could be round, like a glass paperweight. I'll have my report on your desk—' he looked at the date on his watch — 'probably Thursday. No, make it Friday. We've got rehearsals all this week.'

Malone sighed heavily. 'When did you decide you wanted to be a pathologist, Doctor?'

'I didn't. I've only ever wanted to play in a rock band. My partner makes me do what she calls "a proper job" to help pay the rent. I'm qualified, so I moonlight as a pathologist, when a vacancy crops up.'

When they were back outside, Bugsy turned to Aled. 'If you ever repeat this, son, I'll deny it, but I don't half miss Big Ron.'

* * *

Police Constable Fiona Wainwright had been assigned as family liaison officer to Bob Beacham's widow. Her job was to gather evidence and information from the family to contribute to the MIT's investigation. She explained, in a sensitive and compassionate manner, who she was and why she had come. 'I have to tell you, Mrs Beacham, that Mr Beacham's death is now being treated as murder.'

Barbara Beacham burst into tears. Fiona handed her a box of tissues from a side table, then went into the kitchen and returned with two mugs of tea.

'But I don't understand. They told me Bob died because he hadn't followed proper regulations.'

It seemed the member of staff sent earlier by the Richington-Blythe family had told her, in an insensitive and uncompassionate manner, that it had been an accident, due to Beacham's lack of attention and a flagrant disregard of health and safety procedures.

'It's a shock, finding out that the police think somebody deliberately killed Bob, but it's a relief, in a way. You see, dear, I knew it couldn't have been an accident. My Bob was a good worker. He'd been with the Richington Vale Winery for nearly thirty years. There's no way he would have taken any risks.'

Fiona sipped her tea pensively. 'Why do you suppose the Richington-Blythes suggested that it might have been his own fault?'

'It's obvious, isn't it? They don't want to have to pay out any compensation.' She wiped away a tear. 'What a terrible thing to do to another human being — knock him over the head and suffocate him, in one of those tanks. They will catch who did it, won't they? The police, I mean.'

'We'll do our very best, Mrs Beacham. The senior investigating officer is Detective Inspector Jack Dawes. He's very experienced. He and his team will get to the bottom of it.'

'Will I still get compensation if it's murder and not a work accident?'

'That I can't tell you, but I'll do my best to find out.' Fiona paused. 'Did your husband have any enemies?'

'Not enemies as such. Obviously, as vineyard manager, he had to make sure everyone did their job properly. I expect a few of the lazy ones objected to that, but not enough to kill him, surely?'

'What about in his private life, outside the vineyard?'

Mrs Beacham flushed a little. 'He didn't have a private life apart from me. What are you implying — that he had another woman?'

'Not at all, Mrs Beacham.' Fiona chastised herself for not treading carefully enough. She'd have to get better at this, if she wanted to keep the role. 'I just wondered what he liked to do in his spare time, when he wasn't working.'

'He liked to meet his mates in the pub some evenings, for a few beers. Funnily enough, he didn't like wine.' She smiled, then her eyes filled with tears again. 'I used to tell him off for staying out late. I wish I hadn't now.'

After some more cautious questioning, Fiona prepared to leave, promising to return as soon as she had anything to report. She paused in the hall, admiring a colourful bouquet on the hall table. 'What lovely flowers.'

'They're from the Flower Pot, the florists in the high street. My Bob used to bring me a bunch of roses from there, every Friday night.'

She began to sob again, so Fiona left her to grieve.

* * *

'We had quite a chat, once Mrs Beacham got over the shock.' PC Wainwright was delivering her report directly to DI Dawes. 'Unfortunately, I didn't uncover anything that might be a motive for Mr Beacham's murder. As far as I could see, his daily routine was uneventful. He went to work, came home, ate his dinner and went to the pub.'

'Maybe we should visit this pub,' suggested Malone. 'Have a chat with the barmaid and some of the regulars. There could be aspects of Beacham's life that his wife didn't know about.'

'Are you asking for volunteers, Sarge?' DC Williams was hopeful.

'I think you and DC Fox should pay them a visit. A young couple, out for an evening drink, will be less conspicuous than Inspector Dawes and me, tiptoeing about in our size twelves, trying not to look like coppers.'

* * *

The Blythe Spirit was a typical country pub — oak beams, horse brasses, a log fireplace and not a fruit machine, digital jukebox or pool table to be seen. The name of the licensee over the door was Matthew Brown.

'Good evening, folks.' He put a bowl of nuts on the bar in front of them. 'What can I get you?'

Gemma thought he had a lovely smile. He was certainly very handsome — and looked rather young to be in charge of a pub. Aled was less interested in the landlord than how expensive the drinks would be in a Richington-Blythe pub. He guessed he could claim it on expenses.

'White wine, please,' said Gemma.

'Now, would that be a glass of Richington Vale Chardonnay?' Matt asked.

'Yes, please, and my friend will have one, too.'

Aled had been hoping for a pint of real ale. He wasn't keen on wine. It made him suck in his cheeks — all four of them. But they were on a fact-finding mission, so he nodded.

Gemma started casually, 'Richington Vale — isn't that the vineyard where somebody was murdered recently? I'm sure I read something about it in the *Echo*.'

'That's right. Terrible business,' said Matt.

Rosie, the barmaid, stopped polishing glasses and joined in. There was never much excitement to be had in the village, so a murder was a welcome distraction. 'They say poor old Bob was just going about his business when someone broke in and bashed him over the head. Such a quiet bloke. He used to come in here regularly for a drink and a chat. Now, who would want to do a thing like that?'

'Did he chat to anyone in particular?' asked Aled. Gossip was obviously rife, and he saw no need to correct Rosie's version of events.

'He used to play dominoes with Dave, over there.' She pointed to an oldish man, dozing in the corner. 'He's a regular, all right. Comes in at opening time, blags a drink off anyone who'll pay and stays until we chuck him out.'

Gemma thought it might be worth talking to Dave, if he knew Bob Beacham well. 'Is it too late for some food?' she asked.

'Not at all,' said Matt. 'I'll call the chef to take your order. He's also my partner, Freddy. We run this place together.'

Gemma sighed to herself. *Why do all the charming, good-looking ones turn out to be gay?*

In contrast to Matt, who was lithe and athletic, Freddy clearly worked out. He was built like a weightlifter — heavy and muscular. 'What would you like, folks? Today's special is steak and kidney pie, with mash and seasonal vegetables.'

'Yep, that's for me,' said Aled, who hadn't eaten since breakfast.

'Could I just have a chicken salad?' asked Gemma.

'Certainly. No problem. If you'd like to take a seat, I'll bring it over.'

They sat at the table next to Dave, who woke up and nodded to them. 'Evening.'

'Hello. It's Dave, isn't it?' said Gemma. 'Can we buy you a drink?'

Dave perked up. 'Don't mind if I do.' He signalled to the barmaid. 'Pint of my usual, Rosie, love.' Then he thought he might as well make the most of it. These two clearly weren't locals. 'And a pork pie.'

Cheeky sod, Aled thought, but it was on expenses, so what the heck. He waited until the drinks arrived, then, 'The landlord was just telling us that you were a friend of Bob Beacham, from the winery. Dreadful, what happened to him.'

Dave sank half his pint in a single swallow and shook his head morosely. 'Wrong time — wrong place. Got in the way, didn't he?'

'In the way of what?' Gemma queried.

'The thieves who broke in — although what they planned to pinch from that place is anybody's guess. Bob always reckoned anything worth nicking was up at the Hall.'

'The Hall?' questioned Aled.

'Richington Hall. That bloomin' great mansion, where the Richington-Blythes live.'

'You don't think it was Bob they were targeting, then?'

He looked surprised. 'Why would anyone want to kill Bob? All right, he had short arms and deep pockets when it came to buying a drink, but if all the tight buggers in this village got themselves done in, this pub would be empty. Isn't that right, Rosie?' He held out his glass for a refill.

CHAPTER FOUR

The post-mortem report turned out to be more detailed than anyone who had met Dr Golightly would have expected. Aled noted the main points on the white board in the incident room, next to the SOCOs' photographs of the corpse.

'According to this, the trauma to the back of Beacham's head was caused by something circular with a knob in the centre,' said Bugsy. 'A small metal wheel with a hub. There's a digital representation of the indentations at the bottom of the report. That's helpful.'

'And his head hit the object and not the other way around,' finished Aled.

Jack looked closely at the storage tank in the background of one of the photographs. 'Looks like he fell against the closing valve.'

'You're right, sir. Blood and hair found on the valve were a match for the victim,' agreed Aled. 'But the tox report found no alcohol or drugs in his system, so no obvious reason for him to fall accidentally.'

'So somebody knocked him down?' suggested Gemma.

'They might have got away with an accident, if they'd left it at that,' said Bugsy, 'but carrying him up the ladder and sticking his head in the tank is premeditated murder, in my book.'

'Here comes the science bit.' Aled read from the report. '"The carbon dioxide concentration in the headspace of the storage tank was well over 100,000 parts per million" — that's ten per cent to us maths numpties.'

'And the significance of that is?' prompted Jack.

'"Normal atmospheric carbon dioxide concentration is approximately 0.04%,"' continued Aled. '"At moderate concentrations, carbon dioxide behaves as a simple asphyxiant, replacing oxygen. However, at higher concentrations, carbon dioxide can be directly toxic to central nervous system function, producing narcosis. Breathing carbon dioxide at concentrations greater than ten per cent can produce unconsciousness in less than a minute and, failing rescue, death."'

'I was wrong about Gavin Golightly,' said Bugsy. 'He's done a good job.'

Jack was looking over Aled's shoulder at the report. 'See that box at the bottom, where Doctor Hardacre always initials it with VH? It doesn't have GG in it, does it?'

Aled looked. 'No, sir. It's MC.'

'Huh!' snorted Bugsy. 'Marigold Catwater prepared this. No wonder it's so good.'

'Now that we have forensic evidence supporting murder rather than an accident, I think we should pay the Richington-Blythes another visit.' Jack was well known for his curious 'nose'. Not just because it was slightly off-centre, due to his rugby-playing days, but for sensing when something wasn't quite right. It had served him well as a detective. It had also, on occasions, got him into a good deal of trouble. All the while he'd been at Richington Hall, the 'nose' had been twitching. He was aware of an undercurrent, a dysfunction in the family, that may or may not be connected to the death of Bob Beacham.

'Aled, give Marianne Richington-Blythe a bell. She seems to handle all the admin. Make an appointment for us to speak to the family — all of them.'

* * *

28

Jolyon wasn't at all happy. 'No, Marianne, definitely not! Tell the blasted police we're running a business here. I haven't time to keep saying the same thing over and over because they're too thick to understand it the first time. Tell them Doctor Anstruther oversees the health of my workers, and he's satisfied that Beacham died as a result of an unfortunate accident, brought on by his own negligence. There's no need to discuss it further.'

'Hello? Is that Detective Constable Williams?' Marianne was unsure how her father's pronouncement would be received. 'This is Marianne Richington-Blythe. You phoned to make an appointment to come and speak to the family, concerning the unfortunate death of Bob Beacham.'

'That's right, miss. When would be convenient?'

She took a deep breath. 'I'm afraid my father doesn't see the need to discuss it further. As far as he is concerned, the matter is closed.'

We'll see about that, thought Aled. 'In that case, I'm afraid I must inform you that the intentional, reckless or negligent withholding, hiding, altering, fabricating or destroying of evidence relevant to a potential murder investigation is a criminal offence. It leaves the police with no choice but to caution and arrest all persons of interest and take them to the station to be questioned.'

There was a sharp intake of breath. 'Please leave it with me. I will speak again to Papa.'

When Marianne relayed the message, Jolyon blustered furiously for some minutes about 'blasted police high-handedness' and 'arbitrary exercise of power', then reluctantly agreed to a meeting at the Hall.

* * *

'Well done, young Taffy,' said Bugsy. 'That'll teach old Richington-Blythe he isn't above the law.'

Gemma sniffed. 'You made that up.'

29

Aled grinned. 'Not all of it. If the boss wants to talk to them, it's my job to arrange it, using whatever persuasion is necessary.'

They went mob-handed — Jack, Bugsy, Aled and Gemma. DC 'Mitch' Mitchell drove the police van. Not that Dawes was planning to make any arrests at this stage, but it gave the impression that he might. Aled and Gemma were to note down the salient points during the interviews, and pick up on any nuances. Nobody was to mention what Wendy had told them, because if they did — as Bugsy pointed out — this time next week, she'd be out of a job. Jolyon wasn't the kind of employer who would be influenced by her long service.

Marianne showed them into the sumptuous drawing room. It was occupied by six people — none of whom looked comfortable, despite the opulent seating arrangements. Bugsy smiled to himself. It was a classic 'Agatha' moment when all the suspects are assembled and the detective unmasks the killer. Although why any self-respecting killer would hang around, waiting to be unmasked, instead of catching the next flight to Timbuctoo, he could never fathom.

Marianne introduced them. 'My father, Jolyon, and brother, Sébastien, you have already met. Sandra is my father's wife.'

Gemma was curious that she didn't say 'my stepmother'. No love lost there.

Marianne indicated the lad sitting next to Sandra. 'That's her son, Zack.'

Once again, not 'my stepbrother', thought Gemma. *Bit of a fractured family.*

'Robbie McKendrick is my partner. He's the vineyard engineer and his job is to ensure all the equipment is working properly. This lady—' she pointed to a smartly dressed woman, sitting on the arm of the sofa — 'is Miss Suzy Black.'

Suzy was the only one who smiled, and came forward to shake hands. 'I'm not a member of the family, Inspector. I was hired by Richington Vale three years ago, after answering their advertisement for someone with a qualification from the Institute of Masters of Wine. I'm responsible for quality assurance.'

'It's regarded in the wine industry as one of the highest standards of professional knowledge,' said Sébastien, proudly. 'Apart from testing the quality of our own wines, Suzy leads our wine-tasting classes, gives lectures and judges wine competitions.'

'Thank you.' Aled was busily jotting that down.

Jolyon stood up. 'What's this all about, Inspector? I thought we'd finished with the nonsense about a murder having been committed. I really don't have the time or the inclination to go over it all again, even if you have. No wonder our taxes are so exorbitant.'

Dawes's face darkened. 'I don't think you've quite understood, have you, sir? A member of your staff has, indeed, been murdered and it's my job to find out who did it and why. And as he was one of your longest-serving employees, I'd have thought you might have an interest, too.'

Jolyon strode to the wine table and poured himself a large one. 'We've already discussed this. Beacham fell over and banged his head, and while he was concussed, he climbed up to check the levels in the storage tank and passed out.'

'Don't be any more of an arse than you can help, Jolyon.' Sandra's speech was slightly slurred, indicating that she'd had more wine than the one glass she was holding. 'If it was as simple as that, do you suppose they'd have sent four coppers? And there's another one, sitting outside in a van. Just answer their bloody questions so we can all get on with our lives.'

Gemma quietly made observations about the people in the room, which she would write up into notes later. *Sandra Richington-Blythe. At least twenty years younger than her husband, so almost certainly his second wife. Glamorous in an obvious way, too much make-up, and expensive designer clothes that she somehow looks cheap in.*

She wondered what had happened to Jolyon's first wife — Sébastien's and Marianne's mother. *Zack looks much younger*

31

than his stepbrother and sister, so Sandra must have had him when she was very young. He looks angry and unhappy. Gemma realized these were very superficial observations, but they could be useful later on.

She turned her gaze to Marianne's partner, Robbie. *Swarthy and unkempt. If he were my partner, I shouldn't let him sit on that expensive chair wearing filthy overalls. Looks more like he belongs on a building site than in a winery.* If she had to guess who might have bumped off Beacham, purely on first impressions, her money would be on him. *Maybe he's after the manager's job.* She knew this was unfair and totally without foundation.

Suzy Black, however, is elegant and well-spoken. What do you have to do to become a Master of Wine? And shouldn't that be Mistress? Maybe not. Must be a lot of studying and drinking involved. They don't swallow it though, do they? Bit of a waste. She'd read somewhere that wine tasting can rot your teeth. This lady's teeth were perfect.

While Gemma was doing the background work — what Aled referred to as her 'character assassinations', he was waiting to note down the answers to the bosses' questions. Dawes and Malone worked in tandem on these occasions — a pincer interrogation. Dawes started.

'Mr Richington-Blythe, it may surprise you to know that it is the opinion of the pathologist that Mr Beacham was murdered.'

'Rubbish!' barked Jolyon.

Bugsy took up the questioning. 'You may want to reconsider that response, sir. The post-mortem showed that he was not merely concussed but unconscious when his head was forced into the top of the storage tank. He sustained a cardiac arrest due to asphyxia.'

'Bloody hell, Jolyon, that's awful!' exclaimed Sandra.

'Shut up!' warned Jolyon.

Zack jumped up, clenching his fists. 'Don't you tell my mother to shut up!'

Dawes intervened, genuinely fearing a fight might start. Certainly not a case of happy families here. 'Can anyone think of a reason for someone wanting Mr Beacham dead?'

'Absolutely not,' said Marianne. 'He was the ideal employee — came to work on time, did his job efficiently, then went home to his wife.'

'I take it you've spoken to his wife — I mean widow,' asked Sébastien, who had been uncharacteristically silent until now. 'Maybe she wanted him out of the way. Life insurance, perhaps? She could have paid someone to bump him off.'

'Maybe she's got a lover. Women can be ruthless, when they want shot of you.' Robbie flashed a sideways glance at Marianne.

Dawes and Malone continued questioning, but all they succeeded in doing was stirring up more bile among the family. Sandra carried on drinking, Suzy Black kept checking her phone and Zack looked perpetually like he wanted to punch someone. Robbie and Marianne were pointedly ignoring each other while Sébastien fiddled uneasily with the fringes on his Napoleon armchair.

There was little more to be gained. Dawes spoke directly to Jolyon. 'That's all, sir — for now. There will be other questions, so I must ask you all not to leave the village until further notice.'

* * *

'Charming lot, aren't they?' said Bugsy, when they were back outside in the van. 'I bet Christmas is a barrel of laughs.'

'Are we thinking one of them killed Bob Beacham?' asked Aled.

'If so, it would have to have been one of the men,' said Gemma. 'According to the PM report, Beacham weighed over twelve stone. I'm pretty strong but I doubt I could have carried that kind of dead weight up a ladder.'

Dawes was thinking. 'What about a motive?'

'He was the vineyard manager. Maybe he'd found out something dodgy about the way it's being run. Something they put in the wine that shouldn't be there.' Bugsy didn't know anything about winemaking, but as with anything manufactured, there was always a way you could make it cheaper and sell it pricier. 'He could have been blackmailing them.'

'It's a possibility,' agreed Dawes. 'When we get back to the station, I'll ask Clive and his techie team to look into the business accounts, see if there are any unusual transactions.'

'Apparently, we mustn't call Clive our "techie geek" anymore,' said Gemma. 'He's a "digital forensics specialist".'

'Whatever he's called, he's bloody good at his job,' observed Bugsy. 'If there's any jiggery-pokery with the money, he'll find it.'

'I don't think they'd get away with doctoring the wine,' mused Aled. 'That's what the Master of Wine is there for — to quality assure the product. That Suzy Black looked pretty smart to me, and she's got the qualifications. She'd have detected anything dodgy in a heartbeat, and she didn't look particularly corruptible.'

'I agree,' said Dawes. 'We're back to the MMO of murder investigation — means, motive and opportunity. Means, in this case, was a wine storage tank. Opportunity that allowed the murder to take place — either the main door was unlocked, in which case anyone could have had access, or the killer knew the code. And we have reason to believe our man was wearing a visitor's coat and hat.'

'I wonder what he did with it,' said Aled. 'They might count the passes but they don't count the coats and hats, so they wouldn't know if one was still missing.'

'True, but what we're seriously lacking is a motive. For anyone to become a suspect, we have to establish all three.'

'Back to the drawing board, then, guv. I hope we don't need to go back to the Hall. That fancy chair I was sitting on was designed by someone planning a career as an osteopath.' Bugsy's borderline pastry dependency was kicking in. He fished an elderly sausage roll out of his pocket, brushed off the fluff and bit into it.

CHAPTER FIVE

When Jack got home that evening, appetizing smells were drifting from the kitchen. His wife, Corrie, had just taken a chicken casserole from the oven. He kissed her on the cheek. 'Ooh, lovely. I can just fancy a plateful of that.' He picked up a fork, intending to spear a dumpling, but Corrie rapped his knuckles with her spoon.

'Sorry, darling. It isn't for you. I've made you a cottage pie. This is for Barbara Beacham.'

He put the fork down. 'I didn't know she was one of your customers.'

'She isn't, but she's just lost her husband, and I'm sure she doesn't feel like cooking.'

Corrie Dawes was the owner and head chef of Coriander's Cuisine, a popular and lucrative catering company. Carlene, her deputy, managed Chez Carlene, a bistro with a strong French influence. Together, they ran Corrie's Kitchen, a fast-food takeaway. All three businesses were very demanding, and at one time or another, most of the good citizens of Kings Richington availed themselves of their services. With this in mind, Jack frequently took advantage of Corrie's ear-to-the-ground knowledge of what was going on locally. 'What's the word on the street regarding Bob Beacham?'

Corrie frowned. 'There isn't one, really. Only that everyone feels sorry for Barbara. Both her son and daughter live abroad so she's having to cope alone, until they can get home.' She chewed her lip thoughtfully. 'She says the FLO told her Bob had been murdered. Is that right?'

'No doubt about it. But at the moment, we can't find anyone with a motive.'

Corrie spooned a large dollop of cottage pie onto Jack's plate. 'There isn't much being said about poor old Bob, but if you're looking for gossip, there's always plenty about the Richington-Blythe family.'

'I'm not surprised. They're a pretty poisonous lot. They were at one another's throats, even while we were questioning them.'

'I've really only had dealings with Marianne. She's the one who hires the Cuisine to cater their corporate functions.' Corrie thought for a moment. 'I'm not saying it will help, but you might want to delve more deeply into the relationship between Sandra Richington-Blythe and her husband, Jolyon.'

'Sounds ominous. I try not to get involved in other people's marriages.'

Corrie looked wistful. 'People shouldn't be in too much of a hurry to tie the knot. They should have some fun first. Swallows have the right idea. They mate at a combined velocity of sixty miles an hour. At that speed, there's no time for any unseemly groping in bus shelters or accusations about who is treating whom as a sex object.'

'Right. Then they crap all over your greenhouse roof and bugger off back to Africa.' Jack looked hungrily at his cottage pie with its golden, cheesy crust. 'Any chance of some baked beans and brown sauce with that?'

Corrie laughed. 'You're such a philistine.'

* * *

The night sky above the Richington Vale countryside was cloudless, with just enough moon for someone to see where he was going. From out of the dense woods that flanked Richington Hall, a figure emerged, carrying a backpack. He crept silently down the gently sloping hillside and was soon surrounded by vines, their trunks dark and twisted, like arthritic hands reaching out for help. They stretched endlessly to his left and right, row after row scarcely separated from one another by grassy paths.

Now he walked purposefully, knowingly exactly where he was headed and what he intended to do when he got there. All around him, vines had been meticulously planted and painstakingly cultivated. He noticed a hut hidden away in one corner of the field, where it wouldn't take up valuable planting space. This was where the vine workers kept their pruning knives and various other tools. There was also a bed, so that men who worked shifts could sleep in between. It wasn't kept locked at night, so he stored its location away in his memory as a useful place to hide, if he needed it.

Eventually, he reached a stone monument and stopped. There was a brass plaque on the front, for the benefit of the guided tours. He could just read it in the moonlight.

This vineyard was founded by Air Commodore Sir Donald Richington-Blythe DFC. 1919–1989. Then, on a plain notice below, *Please keep to the path and do not walk among the vines. Thank you for your cooperation.*

The man dropped to his knees. For a moment, it looked like he might be paying his respects, but he'd come for another reason entirely.

He reached into his pocket for a torch and a pruning knife, then he began to make deep cuts in the foot of the nearest vine. From his backpack, he pulled out a garden spray containing a powerful herbicide and sprayed it into the cuts. Moving on to the next vine, he repeated the procedure, until he had poisoned an entire row. Then, he changed direction and worked horizontally, in a straight line.

Satisfied he had completed his task effectively, he made his way back up the hill. This time, when he passed the hut, he could see what appeared to be candlelight flickering inside.

He crept close to investigate, careful not be seen. There were noises — a man and a woman. He was grunting and she was moaning. He dared not get close enough to see who it was, but there was no doubt about what they were doing. But why do it in a grubby hut in the corner of a vineyard at two o'clock in the morning? Not exactly romantic. He shook his head, baffled, then disappeared back up the hill and into the trees.

* * *

It was Saturday night and the Blythe Spirit was rammed. Quiz night always attracted at least ten teams of hopefuls — the prize was a case of Richington Vale Gold Label Chardonnay. Rosie, the barmaid, was rushed off her feet, but quiz night was always lively, so she welcomed the diversion. She also made quite a bit in tips. Right now, she was so hot, her springy ginger curls were plastered to her forehead.

Jim Anstruther, the local GP, had formed a team called the Old Reliables with Patricia Chambers, retired head teacher of Richington Vale Primary School. She had been known to her pupils as 'Potty' Chambers, which was more or less inevitable, given that small children find any kind of lavatorial humour hilarious. The nickname had affectionately endured into retirement.

Both she and Jim were mature quizzers, and between them they could cover most general knowledge subjects, but it was their practice to recruit a couple of younger people to handle questions on popular music, soap stars, reality shows and the like. With most of the usual youngsters away at a music festival, Jim Anstruther had persuaded Sandra and Zack to join the team. He knew that Sandra was an avid soap fan. He had prescribed tablets to help her sleep, after she'd stayed up half the night watching endless repeats. Zack was young enough to know about modern films and music, but he was a reluctant conscript and sat looking sulky for most of the evening. Sandra, on the other hand, was grateful for any opportunity to get away from Richington Hall in general, and Jolyon in particular.

Freddy had come out of his kitchen to assess the number of fish suppers that would be required when the quiz was over. Once a hairdresser, Freddy admired the blonde highlights he had put in Matt's hair. They looked sleek and subtle and toned down the carroty colour. He muttered to Matt out of the corner of his mouth, 'I see we've got Richington Hall royalty in tonight. Are the Old Reliables going to win with Sandra and Zack on their team, d'you think?'

'I doubt if Sandra will be much use. She's been necking the vodka like the Russians are coming up the M4,' Matt muttered back.

Freddy stifled a snigger. 'I bet Zack only came because he thought it was speed dating night.'

Matt picked up the microphone. 'Right, ladies and gents, get your drinks in. The quiz is about to start.'

The result was a three-way draw between the Old Reliables, the Flower Pots — a brother and sister team who owned the florists — and four excitable young women wearing fuchsia-coloured T-shirts and calling themselves the Pink Ladies. The sudden-death question was about anatomy, and Jim knew the answer instantly. He claimed the prize to rowdy accusations of 'Fix!' from the crowd. Given that Sandra and Zack certainly did not want a case of Richington Vale wine, the Old Reliables split it with the Pink Ladies and the Flower Pots.

Jim and Potty left slightly before closing time, as they liked to avoid the mass exodus that Matt's exhortations of 'Time' always generated. Jim lived over his practice at the north end of the village and Potty's thatched cottage was to the south, so they parted at the door of the pub and set off, walking briskly in opposite directions. It was a clear night with plenty of stars and a full moon.

Potty had barely gone fifty yards when she heard a screech of brakes and a crunch. She turned, and her worst fears were confirmed. A car had sped around the dangerous bend by the post office, just as the doctor was crossing the road. He was thrown several feet in the air and fell with a sickening thud.

The car roared off without stopping. Potty ran back to the pub and pushed her way through the noisy, exiting throng. 'Help! Someone ring for an ambulance. Doctor Anstruther's had an accident.'

Her legs were giving way with the shock, so they took her inside, and Rosie fetched her a large brandy. An ambulance and the police were summoned, but when they arrived, Jim Anstruther was pronounced dead at the scene.

Questioning the remaining customers didn't help the constables at all. Nobody apart from Miss Chambers had seen or heard anything before she screamed.

They spoke to the staff. 'Mr Brown, did you hear anything of the accident?'

Matt shook his head. 'Sorry, officer. I was down in the cellar changing a barrel, ready for tomorrow. I only came up when I heard the commotion.'

'And I was in the kitchen, loading all the fish and chip plates into the dishwasher,' offered Freddy.

'How about you, Rosie?'

'It was very noisy. Always is at chucking-out time. Everyone shouting goodnight. I was collecting up the glasses. I didn't hear any cars.'

Unable to find any other witnesses, they took Potty home in a police car with a promise to fetch her next morning and take her to the station to make a statement.

* * *

Sergeant Parsloe sat opposite Patricia Chambers in a comfortable interview room. A uniformed constable put a cup of tea on the table in front of her. When she picked up the cup, it rattled in the saucer. Parsloe realized that the poor soul was still in shock. He was always a bit on edge when he had to question older ladies. It stemmed from the time when, as a young constable, he'd asked the mother of a drug dealer if she knew the extent of the operation. She'd whipped up her vest and said, 'Well, sergeant, the incision was from here to here.'

'I'm so sorry to have to ask you these questions, Miss Chambers. I know you've had a terrible shock, but I need you to tell me, in your own words, what you saw, while it's still fresh in your mind.'

She nodded. 'I understand, Sergeant, but I'm afraid I didn't see very much. I haven't slept a wink, trying to remember something that would help.'

'Just to recap, you say you and the doctor parted company outside the Blythe Spirit and went your separate ways home. Then you heard a squeal of brakes and turned around to see a car hit him. Was it speeding, would you say?'

'Very definitely. That part of the village is a twenty zone. The car must have been doing at least double that. Poor Jim didn't stand a chance.'

'Can you describe the vehicle?'

She frowned. 'Not really. It all happened so fast. It was biggish. Black, I think, or it could have been dark blue. I only caught a glimpse and I wasn't wearing my glasses. At first, I thought it was Zack's. He has one of those big four-wheel drives, I think you call it. But when they took me back inside and gave me a brandy, he and Sandra were still there, so it couldn't have been him, could it? Not many people in the village own a big car. There's the van the florists use to deliver the flowers and plants, but they'd already left.'

Norman asked the next question with little hope of an answer. 'Did you catch any part of the registration number?'

She shook her head. 'No, I'm sorry. You see, by the time I turned around, it was speeding back around the bend by the post office, so I only saw it sideways on.'

'Could you see anything of the driver?'

'No. It was dark apart from moonlight. No street lights in that part of the village. We're very rural.'

Right, and no CCTV for the same reason, thought Parsloe. *We're on a hiding to nothing.* 'Thank you very much, Miss

Chambers. You've been very helpful. The constable here will take your statement, and after you've signed it, he'll drive you home.

'Thank you, you've been very kind.' She regarded him, her head on one side. 'You're little Norman Parsloe, aren't you? I taught you in primary school.'

'That's right, Miss, you did.' *And a right little bugger, I was,* he recalled.

'I have never forgotten any of my little charges. They each had something memorable about them that sticks in your mind. But I confess that lately my mind tends to play tricks. I think I recognize someone, but then I realize that it can't possibly be them. Old age doesn't come alone, Norman.'

After she'd gone, Parsloe sat thinking for a while. The circumstances about this accident worried him. His gut told him it wasn't a straightforward hit-and-run. He went upstairs to the MIT incident room, to speak to Jack Dawes.

CHAPTER SIX

The whiteboard in the incident room was still covered in notes and photos relating to the Bob Beacham murder. So far, their inquiries hadn't uncovered any new information to move the investigation forward. The village of Richington Vale remained a place of interest, so news of the hit-and-run had filtered through to the team, but they didn't consider it had any relevance to the murder investigation. However, when Sergeant Parsloe gave them his version of events, they weren't so sure.

'The thing is, Jack, I don't believe this was a straightforward hit-and-run. Usually with FATACCs, it's kids out of their brains on cheap drink and drugs, who nick a car and roar around the village, late at night. They accidentally hit some poor bugger, panic, drive off, and we find the car burnt out in a field.'

'So how's this one different?' Jack knew that when Norman had a hunch, it usually turned out to have substance. The team gathered around, and Aled brought the sergeant a coffee while he explained.

'For a start, no cars have been reported stolen or found abandoned. But more importantly, the witness says she heard the squeal of brakes before the impact. But the lads who did the forensic collision investigation reckon that from the rubber left on the road, what she heard was the sound of the car cornering hard, then accelerating, not braking. What does that say to you, Jack?'

'That it wasn't an accident, it was intentional. Do we have a reliable description of the vehicle?'

"Fraid not. The best the witness could do was that it was dark coloured, with a wheel on each corner.'

Bugsy was reading the report that Norman had brought with him. 'It says here that the bloke who copped it was Doctor James Anstruther. Wasn't he the quack who insisted Beacham died from an accident? Said it was his own fault, due to lack of proper attention and a flagrant disregard of health and safety procedures — but not murder.'

'That's because the owners of the vineyard employed him, privately, to look after the health of the workers. That way, they could control any adverse issues that cropped up, and avoid bad publicity and investigation,' said Aled.

'Bit of irony, there,' declared Bugsy. 'Now Anstruther's dead, too. And it's turned out to be murder, not an accident.'

Parsloe nodded. 'Tell you what's even more ironic. Just before he was killed, Doctor Anstruther had been taking part in the pub quiz. His team had tied with two of the others for the prize, and . . .'

'Don't tell me, let me guess,' said Bugsy. 'He'd just answered the "sudden death" question.'

Everyone appreciated the irony except Gemma. 'Stop laughing! It's not funny!'

* * *

As with Bob Beacham, the team could find no obvious motive for anyone to want Dr Anstruther dead. Jack decided to dig deeper. 'I think it's time we had look at Doctor Anstruther's records. There could be something in there that provides a clue.'

'I doubt you'll get past his receptionist, sir,' said Aled. 'The general practice patients call her Godzilla. If you ring for an appointment, she makes you tell her all your symptoms in detail, then she decides if you're ill enough to inconvenience the doctor. It was dead embarrassing when I got kicked in the gonads playing rugby. There's no chance she'll allow you to see confidential patient information.'

'Now, listen here, young Taffy,' said Bugsy. 'I'm about to give you another brick in the wall of your police education. There are circumstances that legally oblige a medical practitioner — and in this case, that includes Godzilla — to disclose information to the police. One such circumstance is that imposed by the Road Traffic Act 1988. It's a requirement to provide information from *anyone*, including doctors, which may lead to the identification of a driver alleged to have committed a road traffic offence, particularly one resulting in a fatality. In fact, it's an offence to fail to comply with such a request. We tell Godzilla that our reason for wanting to examine said records is to try to identify the driver who killed her boss.'

In the event, 'Godzilla' was still deeply saddened by the unexpected death of the man who had been her boss for over twenty years. She was happy, she said, to hand over anything that might help to catch the bastard who did it.

Jack and Bugsy took Clive with them, and he soon used his 'digital forensics specialism' to capture all the records on the practice computer, including those relating to the doctor's private patients. While he was doing this, they questioned the receptionist, whose name was Miss Latimer. Even Bugsy wasn't insensitive enough to call her Godzilla.

Predictably, she described him as 'a wonderful man', an 'absolute saint' when it came to working long hours for the benefit of his patients, and no, she couldn't think of a living soul who might want to harm him. And anyway, it was a tragic accident, wasn't it?

When they got back to the station, Clive told a rather different story, when it came to Anstruther's private practice.

'I don't have any medical qualifications but I know a bit about the balance of probabilities.' Oblivious to the rolling eyes, he continued to explain. 'You determine a single event with a single outcome. Then you identify the total number of outcomes that can occur, divide the number of events by the number of possible outcomes, then calculate the probability . . .'

Bugsy's eyes were glazing over. 'Clive, son, if you don't get to the point soon, I'll need another shave.'

Clive grinned. 'Soz, Sarge. What I'm trying to say is that whenever an accident or illness — that's to say an "event" — happened at the Richington Vale Winery, whatever the "outcome", Doctor Anstruther always managed to absolve the management of any responsibility. If you apply the probability rule, that just isn't feasible.'

'Now why would he do that?' asked Jack. 'Surely the Hippocratic Oath required him to uphold specific standards.'

Clive looked a trifle sheepish. 'While I was looking into the medical records, sir, I took the opportunity to hack into the doctor's financial status. He's got shares in the winery — quite a lot, as it happens.'

'So it was in his interests to ensure they made a good profit, and that meant avoiding unwanted interference from the health and safety executive, never mind a legal challenge from any relatives.' Jack was beginning to see a pattern forming.

'What do I always say?' declared Bugsy.

'Follow the money,' everyone chorused.

Gemma was turning this over in her mind. 'Sir, are we saying that someone who was badly injured and didn't get any compensation, because the doctor made it look like it was their own fault, took their revenge by running him over?'

'It's an outside chance, Gemma, but at the moment, we don't have any better leads. By definition, I dare say a lot of those patients will already be dead. All the same, it would help if we had a list of the cases on his files where that could have happened.'

Clive held up a memory stick.

'He's too clever for his own good, that lad,' said Bugsy. 'One day, his head will explode.'

* * *

Following the death of Dr Anstruther, Jolyon Richington-Blythe called a meeting of the Richington Vale board of directors. Marianne prepared six places around the conference room table, with bottles of water, jugs of coffee and notepads. She had ordered sandwiches to be brought in from the restaurant at lunchtime. There were several contentious items on the agenda, so she was anticipating a long and fractious meeting.

As chairman of the board, Jolyon sat at the head of the table with Sébastien on his right and Marianne on his left. At the other end of the table, Sandra sat with Zack on her right and Robbie on her left.

'As your wife, I should sit next to you, Jolyon,' she complained, as she always did at board meetings. She'd had a couple of vodkas to relieve the tedium, so she was already on the wrong side of vociferous.

'Yes, she should,' agreed Zack.

Jolyon sighed. 'Sandra, do we have to argue about this every time we have a meeting? Sébastien, Marianne and I are major shareholders, so it's right that we should sit together. Now, can we get on, please?'

Marianne took a deep breath. 'First item on the agenda — redistribution of the shares held by Bob Beacham and Doctor Anstruther, following their deaths. It's company policy that they are not allocated outside the organization, to any next of kin.' She awaited the shitstorm that would inevitably follow this statement.

Robbie responded instantly. 'They should be distributed equally among everyone on the board. Even in a family business like this, shareholders have legal shareholder rights.'

Jolyon tried to stay calm. 'They also have obligations, Robbie, as defined by the family dynamic. You already receive dividends, and you have the right to vote on any issues as a member of the board. But unless you are a major shareholder, your influence on the management of this company is limited. Sit down.'

'In my opinion,' said Sébastien, 'major shareholders should get an amount proportionate to their existing holding.'

'That isn't fair.' Sandra stood up to make her point, albeit a little unsteadily. 'I should get what you'd have given Dominique, if she'd still been alive.'

Dominique was Jolyon's first wife, and Sébastien's and Marianne's mother. It was from her that they had inherited their warm Mediterranean colouring and dark brown eyes. She had been very beautiful, which was a persistent cause of annoyance for Sandra.

Zack joined the fray. 'My mother has been married to you for fifteen years, but you still don't treat her like your wife.'

The meeting dissolved into chaos, with everyone shouting at once. Jolyon stood up and banged on the table. 'That's enough! As chairman, it's my decision that all the shares should transfer to me for onward distribution as I see fit.' His colour was rising, dangerously.

Marianne spoke quietly to him. 'Papa, remember your heart.' Then, to the others, 'I think we should take a break, for coffee and biscuits.' *And*, she thought, *to give everyone a chance to calm down, as there is worse to come.*

The decision about who should take over from Bob Beacham as vineyard manager was no less controversial.

'It should be Zack,' declared Sandra. 'It's time he had a proper position in this vineyard.'

Jolyon disagreed. 'He's too young. He hasn't had enough experience of growing vines and he's unreliable.'

'That's crap, and you know it!' spat Sandra. 'He's twenty-three and he's been helping out here since he was seven. He knows more than enough to take over.'

Jolyon ignored her. 'I've made my decision. Robbie will take over as vineyard manager. It will fit perfectly with his role as chief engineer. And start as soon as possible, please, Robbie. I've noticed some of the vines in the lower field look like they're dying. I need you to sort it out, before the disease that's causing it spreads to the others.'

'We also need to appoint another doctor, Papa,' Marianne reminded him.

'I've decided I'm going to ask Doctor Dan Griffin. He practises in Kings Richington and doesn't have any private patients, so I imagine he'll be grateful for the chance to make some real money.'

Marianne looked doubtful. 'Isn't his mother Iris Malone? She's married to a police officer — a detective sergeant.'

'I don't see why that should make any difference. Every man has his price. Having a copper in the background could prove very useful.' He looked down at his agenda and scowled. 'Who put this last item on the agenda?'

'I did, Father.' Sébastien braced himself. 'We've had a spectacular offer from a Californian wine company. They want to take over Richington Vale vineyard in a multi-million-dollar deal. They're prepared to keep all our workers on and find jobs for those of us who want to stay. There'll be opportunities in the United States, too. It's a once-in-a-lifetime offer, Father, and I think we should accept.'

Marianne thought Jolyon was going to have a cardiac arrest right there. His face was crimson and his hands were shaking. 'Sell out to a bunch of Yanks? Over my dead body!'

Marianne thought that might well be the case if he didn't calm down. She poured him a glass of water. He reached for it, but knocked it over in his anger. 'Must I remind you? Your grandfather founded this winery in 1953, after he came back from fighting a war and winning a DFC. He was so proud of what he'd achieved, and the respect he'd earned for the Richington-Blythe name.

'You can't spend respect, Father,' said Sébastien. 'The business has been losing money for some time.'

'I say get out now, while we still have something worth selling,' agreed Robbie.

Jolyon was apoplectic. He eyeballed Sébastien. 'If your grandfather knew what you're proposing, he'd spin in his grave.'

'Don't you mean "turn in his urn"?' mocked Sandra. 'You had him cremated, remember?'

'I think we should put it to the vote,' suggested Sébastien.

'Yeah, let's do that,' growled Robbie.

They went around the table.

'Sell,' said Sébastien.

'Sell,' agreed Robbie.'

'Sell,' slurred Sandra. The vodka in her water bottle was starting to kick in.

'Yeah, sell,' Zack echoed his mother.

Jolyon looked beseechingly at Marianne. 'Sorry, Papa,' she said. 'Sell.'

Jolyon stood up and looked at them in much the same way that Julius Caesar must have looked at his pals in the senate, after they'd put the knife in. 'The final decision goes to the major shareholder. My holding exceeds all of yours put together — so we keep Richington Vale vineyard, and that's the end of it.' He walked out.

CHAPTER SEVEN

Suzy Black was on the way to her tasting chamber. There was a new batch of Richington Vale Chardonnay awaiting her attention. As the resident Master of Wine, she was paid to assess the quality and make recommendations for any improvements. She met Sébastien coming from the direction of the boardroom. 'How did it go?' She could tell from his expression that he wasn't pleased.

'Even worse than I expected.' Sébastien was strongly attracted to Suzy, but in the three years she had worked at the vineyard, he'd been unable to establish any kind of relationship other than a purely professional one. She was friendly and polite but nothing more, even though neither of them was committed to a partner. He'd shared with her the details of the potential takeover, and had assured her she would still have a job with the Californian company and almost certainly at an enhanced salary. 'I'm sorry, Suzy. Father was having none of it. He's allowing sentiment to get in the way of sound business sense.'

'It's understandable, I guess. Richington Vale Winery is all he's ever known.'

'I was hoping he'd be thinking about retirement, and this would be the ideal opportunity. His heart isn't strong and he could do with a rest. Added to which, the vineyard isn't making the profit it used to. To sell now would at least give us the best price. The longer he puts it off, the less money it will make.'

'Were any decisions reached about filling the posts of vineyard manager and medical advisor?' Suzy asked. 'Tragic that they both died the way they did — and so close together.'

'Tragic and totally unexpected. Robbie is to take over as vineyard manager, and Father is to ask Doctor Griffin from Kings Richington to take on the medical needs of the workers.'

'I'm sure they'll both do an excellent job.'

'Robbie's first job is to find out what's killing some of the vines. Whatever it is, it will spread, if he doesn't get to the bottom of it soon.'

Suzy frowned. 'That isn't good. If any grapes from diseased vines get into the harvest, even just a few, it could affect the quality of the wine.'

Not for the first time, Sébastien thought how beautiful and sophisticated Suzy looked in her smart suit, with her burnished auburn hair in a tidy pleat. He couldn't help making comparisons with the bottle-blonde lush his father had presented him with as a stepmother. Suzy was as classy as Sandra was common. He guessed Sandra was about ten years older than Suzy, who had, already, done so much with her life. He didn't know anything about Sandra's background, but he doubted it was anything to boast about.

'Suzy, would you have supper with me tonight? To be honest, I need cheering up, after today's debacle.'

She smiled. 'That would be lovely. Where shall we go? We could eat in the restaurant here, or what about the Blythe Spirit? The chef there does an excellent hotpot, so I'm told.'

'I think we could do rather better than that. There's a French bistro in town called Chez Carlene. It has a Michelin star. Let's go there and have something special.'

'And drink wine that doesn't come from Richington Vale Winery.'

They laughed.

* * *

Chez Carlene was busy, as it was every night of the week. The bistro occupied an entire corner of Richington high street, with windows all around. In the summer, there were tables outside under a striped yellow awning. Inside, it was decorated in Parisian style — strongly influenced by Carlene's French partner, Antoine — so that customers might almost be dining on the Left Bank. By day, it was a brasserie, cool and dark with mottled sea-green tabletops and French accordion music playing softly in the background. At night, it turned into a bustling bistro, an urban creation, loud and relaxed, where customers might saunter in wearing a T-shirt and shorts. The menu was simple but superbly executed, with classic fare such as coq au vin with potato gratin or lighter dishes, like an omelette or croque-monsieur. It had taken off immediately, and had captured the imagination of Kings Richington folk, young and old.

Sébastien had booked and the waiter showed them to a table in the window. They ordered wine — a dry, flinty French Sancerre.

'Don't you feel just the teensiest bit disloyal, drinking this?' teased Suzy.

'Not in the slightest. I may order another bottle. I know I tell the punters on the tour that Richington Vale is every bit as good as the French alternative, but I doubt if they believe me. What do you think?'

'As your Master of Wine, I couldn't possibly comment.'

'Seriously, though, Suzy, I am worried about the vineyard. We're losing orders, and what with two deaths that the police are insisting were murders, and now the vines dying off, I wonder how much longer we can carry on.' Sébastien looked momentarily sad. 'It was different when my mother was alive.'

'Tell me about her.'

'Her name was Dominique, and she came from a village outside Bordeaux. Her family made wine from a local vineyard. She was very beautiful and I adored her. She was only forty-nine when she died. Marianne and I were still in our teens. We were devastated.'

'Do you mind me asking what she died from?'

'She contracted some kind of respiratory disease. Back then, she worked alongside Father in the vineyard, sometimes ten hours a day. Doctor Anstruther said it was pneumonia, brought on by working outdoors in all weathers, and not going to him soon enough with a bad cough that she'd developed.'

Suzy topped up his glass. 'What do you think it was?'

He hesitated. 'I believe she got it from the pesticides. Back then, we used highly toxic organophosphates and Maman was out in the vineyard for long hours every day. The manufacturers told Father that all workers who handle such pesticides, or are near areas of pesticide application, risk exposure and illness, but he wouldn't have it. He said it was scaremongering, and if it got out, the workers would leave or make spurious claims against him. He preferred to believe Anstruther's version. Then, to cap it all, a year after Maman died, Sandra turned up on the doorstep, towing Zack, her son — and to everyone's shock, Father married her. To this day, I don't know what he was thinking. She was only half his age. What marriage could survive those odds?'

'And you didn't approve?'

'Well, you've seen her. Would you want her as a stepmother?'

'I repeat — I'm only your Master of Wine, I couldn't possibly comment on family matters. That's well above my pay grade.'

The food arrived then and they moved on to more cheerful topics, but it left Suzy with much food for thought.

* * *

That night, someone broke into the offices of Leggett, Leggett & Fallover, Estate Agents & Solicitors. Their building occupied a prominent position, halfway down the main street of Richington Vale village, next door to the Flower Pot. As luck would have it — bad luck — Peter Leggett, the senior partner, was working late. He was upstairs in his office, drafting a particularly lengthy and confidential petition on behalf of a member of the Richington Vale Winery. He was rewarded for his diligence with a resounding whack on the head.

As soon as he was able, he called the police. By the time Sergeant Parsloe and his uniformed officers arrived, Leggett was sitting with a large whisky and holding a bag of frozen peas on a burgeoning lump.

'Did you see who did it, sir?'

'No, I was leaning over my computer, concentrating on some important documents, when he crept up on me from behind. That's the last I remember until I came round, lying on the floor.'

'How did he get in?' asked Parsloe.

'There's a broken window downstairs, Sarge. Constable Johnson has put tape around it, in case of fingerprints.

'Is anything missing?' Parsloe was looking around the room, but it didn't look like your average opportunist burglary, where items are strewn about the room, lamps turned over and drawers pulled out. This was a targeted break-in.

'I haven't had a chance to look properly, but I don't think anything obvious has been stolen. Any valuables are locked in the safe overnight. It doesn't look like it's been tampered with. It's a high-security model, so I doubt your common-or-garden safe-cracker would be able to get into it. Not without explosives, anyway.'

Parsloe closed his notebook. 'I'll get our fingerprint experts around in the morning. In the meantime, try not to touch anything.'

As the police were leaving, Leggett said, 'There's just one thing, officer. It looks as though the burglar tried to get into my computer.' He pointed to the screen. 'That isn't the program I was using before I was knocked unconscious. I was working on some confidential files for the Richington-Blythes.'

'So chummy was after information, rather than valuables. That's very helpful, sir. My advice is to take some paracetamol and try to get some sleep. We'll be in touch.'

CHAPTER EIGHT

Sergeant Parsloe wouldn't normally have considered it necessary to discuss a burglary with the MIT, but because of Jack's interest in the Richington Vale Winery, he thought it worth mentioning.

Jack was interested. He had two unsolved murders, and incidents connected in some way to the Richington-Blythes were cropping up on a regular basis. Too often to be a coincidence, and anyway, Jack didn't believe in coincidences. 'Were there any fingerprints?'

Norman shook his head. 'No. Only the staff. Chummy was wearing gloves.'

'What? Even when he was trying to type on a keyboard?' Clive was doubtful. 'What about on the actual keys?'

'Forensics tried that, but there were too many other prints to get anything useful, apparently.'

'And it was definitely a bloke?' Bugsy had arrested some pretty powerful women in his time — women quite capable of clocking you over the head, if the mood took them.

'We're assuming so. CCTV was inconclusive. There's none in the rural part of the village but there is one outside Leggett's. The burglar was wearing a black hoodie and a ski mask. Could've been a man or a woman, but we decided it was a man from the way he ran.'

'Yeah,' agreed Bugsy. 'Women do run funny, now you come to mention it.'

'Only because our legs are shorter,' said Gemma. 'I bet I could outrun you, Sarge.'

'A dripping tap could outrun me, DC Fox. I'm built for comfort not speed.'

Clive's thoughts, as always, were on whatever the burglar had been looking for on the solicitor's computer. 'Sir, shall I see if I can hack into Peter Leggett's system? I might be able to find out what the burglar was looking for.'

Jack shook his head. 'No, Clive, absolutely not. Those files are confidential between Leggett and his clients. It would be illegal, not to say unethical, for the police to hack in without some kind of warrant.' He grinned. 'Let me know what you find.'

* * *

Cynthia Garwood, Chief Superintendent George Garwood's wife and self-styled psychotherapist, was chairperson of the Inner Wheel Club. Since she had been voted in, the club had done magnificent work, raising funds for deserving charities. Their motto of 'Friendship and Service' also applied to her relationship with Corrie Dawes. Their friendship was unequivocal, and the service happened whenever she needed Corrie to cater for a special occasion, as she was hopelessly inept when it came to cooking anything. This was one of those occasions. She telephoned. 'Hello? Is that you, Corrie?

'Well, if it isn't, these cargo pants are a remarkably good fit. What do you want, Cynthia?'

'What are you doing on Saturday afternoon?'

'What am I always doing on Saturday afternoons? Cooking for what seems like the figurative five thousand. Why, what do you want me to do?'

57

'I'm holding a fundraising luncheon to raise money for "Friends of the *Echo*". It's their donations that keep the paper going. D'you think you could rustle up a buffet luncheon for fifty — plus a few dignitaries?'

'What?' Corrie yelped. 'The *Echo* is a scurrilous rag, and the editor is an unprincipled hack with a distinct bias against the police and the government. I doubt he's got fifty friends.'

'That's what George said. I take the pragmatic view that it's better to have him on the inside of our tent peeing out, than outside, peeing in. If the press is on our side, there's a better chance of the police getting more positive publicity. Added to which, we sometimes need the editor's cooperation with things like finding missing persons, errant dogs and not giving the game away to villains, until the cops are ready to nick 'em. What do you say, Corrie?'

'OK. I'll get Carlene to help. Where are you holding this bunfight?'

'In the events suite of the Richington Vale Winery. You've catered there before. It's a glorious venue with incredible views out over the vineyards. Sheila and Miles Barton from the Flower Pot are doing the floral decorations and Jolyon Richington-Blythe is letting us hire the vineyard at cost and donating the wine — very generous. Especially as they've had a couple of nasty incidents recently.'

'Yes, poor Barbara Beacham's husband was suffocated in a wine tank and the vineyard doctor got run over. Let's hope that's an end of it. You know what we're like for walking into trouble. What sort of buffet do you want?'

'I'll leave it to you. You know the facilities there, so anything that will go with their award-winning sparkling Chardonnay — and isn't so expensive it wipes out all the profit — will be perfect.'

* * *

When Jack got home that evening, Corrie was planning the buffet and listing the ingredients she would need.

'Cynthia's having a charity do at the Richington Vale Winery on Saturday. Carlene and I are catering a hot buffet. Have you finished your inquiries there? Only, I don't expect she'll want the place crawling with coppers, especially as the editor of the *Echo* will be there.'

Jack looked to see what was in the oven for supper. 'We've finished with the crime scene, but not with the Richington-Blythes. My gut tells me there's more going on there than they're letting on. My gut also tells me that I'm faint for lack of nourishment. Is that duck I can see cooking? Port and redcurrants?'

'Ready in half an hour. So it's OK if we take over the events suite?'

'Yep. Just stay out of trouble. There's always mayhem when the three of you get together.'

* * *

It was certainly an excellent venue. Corrie had been impressed with the facilities whenever she had catered there. There were rumours that the winery wasn't doing so well. It certainly didn't look like that to her. The events suite was elegant and well-appointed, with strategically placed vases showing Dionysus, Greek god of fruitfulness, vegetation and wine, holding aloft bunches of grapes. She recognized the work of Sheila Barton. She really was good. She and her brother, Miles, had only arrived in the village a couple of years ago, and between them they'd built up a good business. He worked in the market garden providing plants and flowers for Sheila to sell in the shop. It was a lucrative and symbiotic partnership.

The vineyards looked green and healthy, apart from one field where Corrie noticed the vines were brown and shrivelled. She wondered what had happened. No doubt the owners knew and were dealing with it. Maybe they had deliberately destroyed it, to make way for new growth. She knew nothing about viticulture, although she knew plenty about the end product and what wines to serve with various meals.

As guest of honour, the editor of the *Echo* made a dreary speech, including a rather protracted vote of thanks to the Inner Wheel ladies and the excellent caterer, 'despite the fact,' he joked, 'that she's married to a copper.'

'Blummin' cheek,' muttered Corrie.

'You can say that again.' Rosie the barmaid, her flaming ginger hair scrunched up in a topknot, was standing beside her, holding a tray of drinks. She'd been co-opted from the Blythe Spirit to help serve the wine. 'He brings his cronies into the pub and expects Matt and me to run around waiting on him. Never so much as a "Have one yourself, Rosie." Tight as a frog's bum, that bloke — pardon my French. Speaking of French, that's Mr Jolyon Richington-Blythe over there, with his second wife, Sandra — mutton dressed as lamb. His first wife, Dominique, was French. That's why both the children have French names. Of course, I was only a toddler when she died, but I remember she always smelled nice and had sweets in her pocket for us village kids. She was a lovely lady, and I mean a real lady. Not like that flashy piece Mr Richington-Blythe is married to now. Look at her, all airs and graces but common as muck. What my gran would call "all fur coat and no knickers". There's a gold digger if ever I saw one. I feel sorry for Zack. Still, I can't stand here chatting. I've got to give away these drinks. D'you want one?'

Corrie declined. She smiled to herself. There were certainly some lively characters in Richington Vale.

Over by the glass cabinet, full of wine trophies, Sandra Richington-Blythe slipped her arm through Jolyon's, and with a fixed smile she hissed through gritted teeth, 'If I don't get a decent drink soon, I'm going home.'

Jolyon hissed back, through equally gritted teeth and the rictus of a smile, 'Shut up and try to behave like the wife of a gentleman.'

'I would if I could find one.' She snatched a glass from Rosie's tray as she passed and knocked it back in one. 'This stuff's tasteless piss. Beats me how you've made so much loot out of it.'

'I shan't have the "loot" for much longer, if you keep spending it on cases of vodka and designer frocks that are too young for you.' He looked her up and down. She was spilling out of a black satin cocktail dress that was far too short for her. 'You look like an overstuffed bin bag.'

'Bastard!'

'Bitch!'

* * *

Up on the platform, the editor was droning on. Patricia 'Potty' Chambers, a life member of the Inner Wheel, was thinking what a good effort the fundraising had been. The buffet had been superb, but she wasn't a fan of the sparkling Chardonnay, even if it had won awards. In her opinion, it was fizzy pop with a fancy label. She'd had the foresight to bring a hip flask, filled with her favourite cognac.

Looking around, there were people she knew well, some she didn't know at all and a few that she only recognized vaguely. They could live next door, but her incipient dementia wouldn't bring them to mind. It was a spasmodic thing. Sometimes, she was sharp as a needle, like when she'd been taking part in the pub quiz. But now, one person in the room was particularly taxing her memory. She simply couldn't remember the name, but she was certain they had met. It might have been some time in the past. Although, once you reached a certain age, it was difficult to tell exactly which bit of the past it was — yesterday or years ago. It was no use. There was only one way to find out, or it would irritate her for weeks.

She went across. 'Hello. Wonderful turnout, isn't it? I'm Patricia Chambers. I used to be head teacher at Richington Vale Primary. You must excuse me, but I'm sure I know you from somewhere. I simply can't bring your name to mind.'

The reply was curt and didn't offer a name. 'What makes you think we've met?'

'It's just a senior moment, but if you don't mind me saying, it was that scar on your neck that somehow triggered my memory. This must seem very rude, but I've no idea why. Of course, it could have been some time ago. No doubt it will come to me, eventually.'

* * *

It took some time to clear up the clutter. The more wine people drank, the messier they seemed to get, until there were glasses and plates of leftover food abandoned all over the suite. Otherwise, a good time was had by all, and the 'Friends of the *Echo*' coffers had benefitted considerably. Marianne, together with the staff from the restaurant and Rosie, helped tidy everything and load the serving dishes into the Coriander's Cuisine van. Sheila and Miles had dismantled the Dionysus displays and taken them home.

They were about to leave when Cynthia spotted Potty asleep in a comfortable chair by the window. They went across to rouse her.

'The sun must have made her drowsy and she's nodded off, bless her. Come on, now, Miss Chambers. Time to go home.' Cynthia shook her shoulder gently. When Potty didn't respond, she shook it more vigorously. Still no response. She felt for a pulse. White-faced, she turned to Corrie and Carlene. 'I think she's dead.'

'She can't be,' said Carlene. 'She's just had a bit too much of the falling-down water.' She took one of Potty's hands and rubbed it. 'Come on, love. Let's get you out into the fresh air.' Carlene looked more closely. 'What's that white stuff at the corner of her mouth?' She detected a faint smell of almonds. She hadn't been around Inspector Jack and Sergeant Bugsy all these years without knowing what that meant.

'Looks like she's been swigging something out of this.' Corrie picked up Potty's flask from beside her chair, where she'd dropped it. She unscrewed the lid and sniffed. 'Smells like brandy.' She went to taste it.

'No! Don't touch that, Mrs D,' Carlene warned. 'I think she's been poisoned with cyanide.'

Startled, Corrie pulled out her phone. 'I'm calling Jack.'

'Blimey, that's three stiffs now,' said Carlene. 'Richington Vale must be jinxed.'

CHAPTER NINE

Fifteen minutes later, Jack, Bugsy, Aled and Gemma were on the scene.

Jack took Corrie to one side. 'I thought you promised to stay out of trouble. You're out of my sight for five minutes and suddenly a poisoned corpse turns up. It might have been you.'

'That's untrue, unfair and unlikely. I'd been out of your sight for several hours, not five minutes, and we only found the body — we didn't have any part in her death. So how might it have been me? You're such a worryguts.'

'Do you know who she is?'

'Cynthia says she's Patricia Chambers, one-time headmistress of Richington Vale Primary School and life member of the Inner Wheel.'

'Wasn't she the old dear who witnessed the hit-and-run?' Bugsy and the others had caught up.

'That's right,' said Aled.

'Do you think the two murders are connected, sir?' asked Gemma. 'It could be a motive. Someone's scared Miss Chambers saw more than she realized of the hit-and-run and might remember it later, so they shut her up.'

'We mustn't jump to conclusions,' Jack cautioned. 'We don't know how or when she died, until the pathologist gets here. But I'm inclined to agree with Carlene's assessment, that she was poisoned with cyanide.'

Dr Golightly, or 'Gormless Gavin', as Bugsy had nicknamed him, arrived late, having been in the middle of a gig. Underneath his SOCO suit, he was wearing a fluorescent green vest with *Necrotic Nightmare* printed on the front, camouflage pants held up by a studded belt, and combat boots under protective covers. The long orange hair had been hastily crammed inside the white plastic hood of the protective suit, so his head looked like a badly stuffed cushion. He was clearly miffed at being dragged off stage, even though it was only talent night at the Richington Parva Cocoa Rooms. As he came through the door, Miss Catwater handed him his pathology bag of tricks in exchange for his guitar, which he had deemed much too precious to leave in the car. She held it away from her, like a wet umbrella.

Golightly knelt beside the body and opened his bag. After a while, when he hadn't spoken, Jack became impatient. 'What can you tell me, Doctor?'

'What do you want to know, Inspector?'

'I was hoping for an estimated time of death.'

'Do you smoke?'

'No.'

'Drink?'

'Not on duty, thanks.'

'Then I reckon you could have around forty years. That's assuming you aren't hit by a bus.' He returned to his deliberations.

Jack couldn't decide if he was being sarcastic or serious.

'Was she poisoned, Doc?' asked Bugsy.

Golightly looked at Miss Catwater, who was placing Potty's flask in a plastic bag. 'What d'you reckon, Marigold?'

'Obviously, we'll run a tox screen, Doctor, but from first indications — bitter almond odour emanating from the victim and the presence of pink lividity, I'd agree — acute cyanide poisoning. From the rigor mortis, I'd say she's been dead between two and four hours. We can confirm the presence of cyanide in the body by a colorimetric test, followed by a laboratory analysis, using gas chromatography. And I shan't be surprised if we find dregs of prussic acid in this flask.'

Bugsy nodded at Marigold. 'She's good, isn't she?'

'Well, the cyanide won't have been in the food or wine,' said Corrie, 'because if it had been, we'd all be dead.'

'Here's the sixty-four-dollar question,' said Jack. 'Was it already in her flask when she got here, or did someone put it in there after she arrived? If so, why?'

Marigold stood up and collected her paraphernalia. 'Not my department, Inspector. As Doctor Hardacre has often told you, we do the "how" and the "when". The "why" is down to you. Come along, Doctor Golightly.'

Aled and Gemma managed to speak to those people who hadn't yet left, but most had already gone home. Jack knew they could get a guest list from Cynthia, though it would take a great deal of time and manpower to track them all down. And even then, he suspected nobody had seen anything useful, and even if the killer was among them, they'd hardly be likely to give themselves away. Not with the kind of luck he was having lately.

* * *

When they returned to the incident room, Clive was waiting for them. 'I obeyed your orders, sir, and I definitely didn't hack into Peter Leggett's system.'

'Good man,' said Jack. 'So you aren't able to tell us about anything you found?'

'No, sir. I'm especially unable to tell you that the document Leggett was working on when he was bashed over the head was a divorce petition.'

'Jolyon Richington-Blythe wants shot of his missus,' assumed Bugsy.

'Not quite, but close,' said Clive.

'I bet I can guess,' said Gemma. 'It's the other way around. Sandra is divorcing Jolyon and wants a hefty pay-off.'

'Dead right. And if she gets what she's asking for, it'll ruin him,' said Clive. 'The Richington Vale vineyard isn't doing as well as everyone thinks. You'll have read my report from when you asked me to look into their business accounts, after the manager was murdered, sir. Lots of debt, and orders have dropped right off.'

'Is Sandra Richington-Blythe likely to get what she wants?' asked Jack.

'Well, sir, I don't have any legal training, but she's been married to him for fifteen years, and she does have a trump card up her sleeve.'

'Which, of course, you can't tell us about, because you didn't hack in,' said Jack.

'Correct, sir. But if I *were* able to tell you, you'd be surprised to learn that the father of Zack, born twenty-three years ago, is Jolyon Richington-Blythe.'

They were digesting this information when Gemma said, 'That can't be right. According to my notes, his first wife was still alive twenty-three years ago. So how could Jolyon have fathered a son with Sandra?'

The men in the room looked at her pityingly.

'I think we should have a private chat with Sandra,' decided Jack. 'There's more going on in that family than they want us to find out. With a bit of luck, we'll discover a connection to all three of our murders. Bugsy, you're with me.'

* * *

Sandra Richington-Blythe opened the door. 'Not you again,' she said, unceremoniously. 'What do you want this time?' She was wearing a garish floral lounge dress, flowing skirt down to the floor but with plenty of cleavage and rows of clanking beads. Normally, Bugsy was quite partial to a bit of bosom, but on this woman, it seemed distasteful to look. She had a half-empty glass in her hand.

They showed their warrant cards. 'We'd like to ask you some questions, madam.'

'No. It isn't convenient.' She went to close the door. 'Come back when you've made an appointment. Ring Marianne.'

Bugsy put his boot in the door. 'No, I'm afraid it doesn't work like that. Either we come in and speak with you now, or we arrest you on suspicion and take you down to the station.'

'On suspicion of what?' she shrilled.

'I don't know yet, madam, but we'll think of something, if you continue to be uncooperative,' said Jack.

She went inside but left the door open for them to follow her. Bugsy closed it behind them. She didn't take them into the opulent drawing room but into a small sitting room, off the hall. She went across to the drinks cupboard and topped up her glass with neat vodka. Bugsy reckoned she must keep a supply in every room in the house. Probably even in the loo.

She took a good slug. 'I know what this is about. Peter Leggett phoned me. He said he was working on my divorce petition when someone broke in and knocked him out. Was that one of your heavies?'

'Certainly not,' said Bugsy, offended. 'We're police officers. We're not in the habit of breaking and entering and committing common assault.'

'Well, who was it then?'

'We don't know yet, madam. Uniformed police officers attended the scene and they're still investigating.'

She shrugged. 'Well, it's not important. Everyone will know sooner or later.'

'May we ask why you're seeking a divorce?' asked Jack. 'You don't have to answer that, if you'd rather not.'

She took another gulp of vodka. 'No, I don't mind. I'm getting out of this dump but I'm not going empty-handed. Not after fifteen years of being treated like a cheap tart. This whole family behaves like Zack and I are scum. Seb and Marianne look down their noses at us because we don't talk like them, with their toffee-nosed French accents.' Her speech was becoming indistinct. She went to refill her glass yet again.

Any minute now, she'll be swigging it straight from the bottle, thought Bugsy. 'You might want to ease off on that, madam,' he suggested.

She turned on him. 'Don't you start! That's all I ever get. *You're drinking too much, Sandra. Count the units, Sandra.* I've tried counting the bloody units, but after ten it gets confusing.' She burped. 'I understand that alcohol in excess can cause untold misery, not to mention humping the empties down the bottle bank before the bastards can count them. And I see them sneering when I don't use the right cutlery and don't drink the snobby piss they call wine. Well, I've had enough of it.' She refilled her glass, almost to the brim. 'The last straw was when Jolyon refused the takeover from California. We'd all have been in the money then, but the stupid sod turned it down. Couldn't possibly sell the vineyard that His Royal Bollocks, Air Commodore Sir Blinking-Blythe, passed down to him. Oh, no. He'll carry on until he's run the place into the ground and then I'll get nothing, so I'm getting out now, while there's still a few quid left to divvy up.' She'd been pacing up and down, but her knees were wobbly, so she sank into an armchair. 'I suppose you know Jolyon is Zack's dad?' She put a finger to her lips. 'Shh! Don't want Zack and the others to find out. Not yet.'

'How did that come about, madam?' asked Jack.

'Can you please stop calling me "madam"? It reminds me of a time I'd rather forget. Jolyon was on a wine seminar. He was staying in the hotel, where I was working as a cocktail waitress. That's what they liked to call it, but the manageress expected you to do a bit more than that, if you wanted to keep your job.' She burped again, audibly, several times. 'I was very young, only eighteen. I thought Jolyon was so cool and sophisticated. He was good-looking too, in those days, not the bald-headed old pot-belly he is now. It was the same old story. You must have heard it a million times, occife— *hic* — officers. By the time I found out I was pregnant, Jolyon was long gone. I traced him from the hotel register. Obviously, he didn't want to know, said the baby

could be anybody's. Bleedin' cheek! Anyway, to cut a short
. . . story . . . long—' she was muddling up her words, now,
so Jack didn't think the interview would last much longer
— 'DNA proved Zack was his, so he started sending me
money. Said he'd divorce his wife when the children were
grown up, but he never did. Then Dominique got ill. After
she died, I turned up here and told him I'd stir up a right
royal shitstorm if he didn't marry me, so he did.' She tried to
stand but fell back down. 'Sergeant, could you pass me that
bottle over there?'

Bugsy went to get it, but when he turned around, Sandra
had passed out. They let themselves out.

CHAPTER TEN

Back at the station, they discussed the new information, and interesting though it was, nothing Sandra had told them seemed to have an obvious connection with the murders of Beacham, Anstruther and Patricia Chambers.

'Well, I feel sorry for her,' said Gemma. 'It must be rotten living in an atmosphere where everyone looks down on you because you're common. She's over forty — she needs to get out while she still has some life ahead of her. I hope Leggett gets her a good settlement. She's earned it.'

'That's your feminist law degree talking, young Gemma. I reckon she needs to stop drinking first,' observed Bugsy.

'I don't know, Sarge, I think I'd drink if I had to live with that lot,' said Aled.

'Where do we go from here, guv?' Bugsy wanted to know.

'We keep asking questions, until we get some answers.'

'I've got the latest report from SOCO here, sir,' said Aled. 'Incidentally, did you know the Home Office now has an Evidence and Biometric Identity Management department? Anyway, they've finished analysing Miss Chambers' flask and there were only her fingerprints on it. But they did find a residue — most probably, they say, from a glove with a polyurethane coating. Assuming Miss Chambers wasn't in the habit of filling her flask wearing gloves, they would most likely have belonged to her murderer.'

'Are these gloves special enough to be traceable?' asked Bugsy.

'Not really, Sarge. There must be millions of 'em. But what I found interesting was that polyurethane is considered the ideal coating for cut-resistant gloves. I quote, "Such gloves are tough, long lasting and very thin. Good puncture resistance without being too bulky. Ideal for precision work and general sharp handling."'

'I see where you're going with this, son,' said Bugsy. 'They're the sort of gloves that might be found in a vineyard, to protect the hands of the workers pruning the vines.'

'I've seen those pruning knives,' said Jack. 'They have a curved blade and they're bloody sharp.'

Gemma was puzzled. 'Are we saying a vine worker poisoned Miss Chambers' flask?'

'Not necessarily,' said Jack. 'It could be anyone with access to the gloves.'

'Another interesting fact in the report on the flask is that they found traces of hydrogen cyanide, also called prussic acid. It's a chemical compound produced on an industrial scale, and it's used in the vineyard as a fumigant against insects. It's colourless, highly toxic and with a bitter almond odour.'

'From that, I think we can safely assume that her cognac was poisoned *after* she arrived at the winery and not before.'

'So our suspects include everyone who works there, the Inner Wheel ladies and all the other folk who were at the "Friends of the *Echo*" fundraising bash,' said Bugsy.

'Don't forget the catering staff,' said Jack, grimly.

* * *

Needing a break from the worrying events that seemed to be overwhelming the winery, Marianne and Sébastien went into Richington Vale village. They decided to lunch at the Blythe Spirit, where they could sit and chat, an opportunity that had been sadly lacking of late. They ordered coffee and sandwiches and settled in the corner by the window for a private, brother–sister catch-up.

'Seb, what's happening to us? Papa is angry all the time, Sandra is always drinking and Zack gets more and more withdrawn. And when he does speak, he seems to hate us all. As for Robbie, I scarcely see him these days. I don't even know where he is half the time.'

'Robbie is the vineyard manager now, Mari. He's bound to be busy with extra responsibilities. He'll be in the vineyards, managing the picking, now harvesting is starting.'

'In the middle of the night? I wake up and he isn't beside me or anywhere in the apartment. Then, in the morning, he's back.'

'Have you asked him about it?'

'Yes. He just said that sometimes he finds it hard to sleep, worrying about money, so he goes for a walk.'

'Well, there you are, then. Perfectly reasonable explanation. Loads of folk do that.'

'But he didn't used to have a problem. It only started recently.'

Freddy, the inveterate gossip, came over with their coffee and sandwiches. 'Seb, Marianne, how lovely to see you. How are you guys doing? From what I've heard, things have been a bit lively — or should I say, deadly — up at the winery. First Bob Beacham, now Potty Chambers.'

'That's right, Freddy,' said Sébastien. 'But the police are on it.'

Freddy wasn't about to be fobbed off. 'I heard about poor Miss Chambers. People are saying she was poisoned at one of your events. Terrible news. She was a lovely old girl, often popped in for a brandy. Staunch supporter of the pub quiz, too. Mind you, when Doc Anstruther was run over, that was the end of the Old Reliables. It happened right outside here. Frightened everyone to death. You're not safe in your own village these days. Anyway, I can't stand here gossiping. I've got twenty hotpots to prepare by opening time tonight. Nice to see you.'

'Do you suppose everyone in the village is talking about us?' Marianne pushed down the plunger of the cafetière and poured the coffee.

'It'll blow over, once the police get to the bottom of it. Listen, Mari, I want to tell you something. It's about Suzy.'

'What about her? Please don't tell me she wants to leave because of the problems we've been having. She's the only friend I have at the moment.'

'No, nothing like that. I've decided to ask her to marry me.'

'Seb, that's wonderful! Suzy is perfect for you.'

'The way Father is behaving, and with the vines dying for no reason, the orders are falling off, rapidly. If Richington Vale goes into liquidation, she'll move on and I'll have lost her.' He picked up a sandwich and toyed with it, as if bracing himself to reveal more. 'The thing is, Mari, a wine company in Napa Valley has offered me a job. It's a chance in a lifetime. Suzy is a Master of Wine, so I'm sure she could get a job there, too. I want her to marry me so we can go as husband and wife. What do you think?'

'Go for it. It's time you settled down. *Tu ne rajeunis pas.*'

Seb laughed. 'Neither are you, *ma petite soeur*. Isn't it about time you and Robbie tied the knot?'

Marianne's face fell. 'That's never going to happen. I don't think Robbie will be around for much longer.'

* * *

That night, when Bugsy got home, his stepson, Dan Griffin, had called in for a chat. Iris was taking a fragrant steak and kidney pie from the oven. Bugsy and Dan did the awkward man-hug thing before they sat down to eat.

'Good to see you, son. To what do we owe the pleasure? It must be important — I know your evenings are busy.'

'Yep. I always seem to be taking the kids to football practice, dance class, stuff like that. But I need to talk to you about Richington Vale Winery, Mike.' Danny was probably the only person in the world, other than Iris, who called Bugsy by his real name.

'*Aah.*' Bugsy had put a forkful of very hot pie in his mouth and was temporarily speechless.

'Mum says you already know about Doctor Anstruther getting killed in a hit-and-run. The MIT are treating it as a murder, she said. Well, Anstruther was the doctor who oversaw the health of the vineyard workers, and Jolyon Richington-Blythe has asked me to take over from him.'

'I don't want him to do it,' said Iris. 'Neither does Cheryl. It sounds dangerous to me. After all, the police haven't found out who ran Doctor Anstruther down yet. There are more important things in life than money.'

'Mum, the only people who say that are the ones who haven't got any. But it isn't the money I'm concerned about. Mike, when Richington-Blythe summoned me to talk terms, he made a few stipulations that bothered me.'

Bugsy had now swallowed the hot pie and drank some cold beer to soothe his blistered mouth. 'I think I know what you're going to say, Danny. Your job would be to make sure that if any of the workers had an accident or contracted a disease, it would always be recorded as their own fault, due to negligence or a disregard for health and safety rules. The company would never be held responsible. And even if some brave soul did try to mount a claim, they'd have a struggle with medical evidence against them.'

'That's right. I couldn't possibly sign up to that. No self-respecting doctor could, no matter what the salary.'

'Anstruther did. He had shares in the vineyard.'

Dan was shocked. 'That's appalling. If he hadn't died, I'd have had to report him to the GMC.'

'The tech lads back at the station are going through his past vineyard patients. It'll be interesting to see what they turn up. Richington-Blythe could end up facing a charge of criminal negligence.'

'I'll tell Richington-Blythe I couldn't possibly accept the job on his terms,' said Dan. 'Thanks, Mike.'

'Good man.' Bugsy took another forkful of pie, and this time he blew on it.

CHAPTER ELEVEN

Monday nights were quiet in the Blythe Spirit. Vine workers, who made up much of the custom, were either recovering from the excesses of the weekend or had spent all their money until they got their wages on Friday. Sheila and Miles from the Flower Pot were in, enjoying a bottle of wine, and so was Peter Leggett, having only to walk a few yards to get home. Dave occupied his usual spot, over by the fireplace, hoping someone would offer to buy him a drink.

Zack sat nursing a pint and looking dejected. His face lit up as soon as Rosie came down to his end of the bar. 'Are we on for tonight, babe?'

She smiled and pretended to wipe his bit of the bar with her cloth. 'Yes, all right. After closing time. I'll tell Dad I had to stay late to wash glasses and clear up. We'll have to be careful, though. He's getting suspicious.'

'I don't see why we have to keep our relationship secret from your dad. What's he got against me?'

'You're a Richington-Blythe.'

'No, I'm not. Just because my mother married Jolyon and made me take his name, it doesn't make me a Richington-Blythe. He's only my stepfather, and I hate him. I always have. He treats Mum and me like shit. I can't understand why she married him in the first place.'

'My dad says he treats his workers like shit, too. D'you think conditions will improve, now that Robbie McKendrick's taken over as vineyard manager?'

'Doubt it. He's in the old man's pocket, same as Beacham was. Seb and Marianne are OK, but Jolyon holds the purse strings, so we're all his puppets.'

'That includes my dad. He says he'd get out, but there are hardly any jobs around here that aren't connected to the Richington Vale vineyard. The family owns this pub — and most of the other businesses.'

'Well, I'm going to get out. I know enough about vines and making wine to get a job in another vineyard, probably abroad. Somewhere in the sun — Italy or Spain. And when I go, I'm taking you with me. But we're definitely on for tonight, aren't we?'

She smiled coyly. 'All right, but must we always do it in the same place? It isn't very romantic.'

'I know. I will find us somewhere else, I promise.'

'Couldn't we go up to your room at the Hall?'

'No.' He looked uncomfortable. 'I don't want the family to know about you until I'm ready.'

'You're not ashamed of me, are you?'

'Course not. I'll find us somewhere else, but in the meantime, I'll meet you at the usual place. I love you, Rosie.'

'I love you, too.'

* * *

At four o'clock in the morning dawn was threatening to break over the Richington Vale countryside. There was just enough light for someone to see where he was going without a torch. Once again, from out of the dense woods that flanked Richington Hall, a figure emerged, carrying a backpack. He crept silently down the gently sloping hillside, observed the hut in darkness, and was immediately surrounded by vines. This time, they were heavy with fruit. It was early autumn and the harvesting, which is crucial to the success of every vineyard, was about to begin. The grapes were rich in colour, juicy and plump. He pulled one off to taste — it was tightly attached to the stem. A full-flavoured grape, unlike the shrivelled fruit on the vines he had already poisoned. These were the healthy ones that had escaped his deadly ministrations. He knew he couldn't treat every grape in a vineyard as huge as this one, but he could still do enough damage to make them useless for winemaking.

From his backpack, he pulled out a spray containing a cocktail of chemicals designed to rot the fruit as soon as the sunlight hit them. Two hours later, satisfied he had completed his task as effectively as possible in the time available, he made his way back up the hill, just as the sun began to rise. This time, when he passed the hut, a naked man stumbled out, drowsy and unsteady. He leaned against a vine and began to pee. It was too late for the interloper to avoid being seen.

The man stopped peeing. 'Hey! What's your game? You some sort of pervert?' He stared directly into the intruder's face. 'Just a minute. I know you. What the hell are you doing, creeping about at this time of the morning?'

The blade of the pruning knife flashed briefly in the early light, as the trespasser pulled it from his pocket. Without hesitation, he plunged it into the man's chest. Then he dragged him quietly back inside the hut and laid him carefully on the makeshift bed, beside the snoring woman.

* * *

It was still murky inside the hut an hour later, when Sandra woke from her deep sex-and-alcohol-induced sleep. Briefly, she illuminated her watch, then reached a hand across to shake the man beside her. 'Wake up. It's seven o'clock. We fell asleep. We have to get back to the Hall before somebody misses us.' There was no response. She reached closer, to shake him harder, and her hand touched something wet and sticky.

Hastily, she felt for her torch and switched it on. Her fingers were covered in blood. She was lying in a pool of it. Then she saw the pruning knife, sticking out of his chest. Without pausing to grab her clothes, she ran naked through the vineyard, screaming.

* * *

Sandra was hysterical and incoherent by the time she reached the side door of Richington Hall, the same door from which she had tiptoed out the night before. As luck, or fate, would have it, it was Marianne who found her. She had woken to find Robbie still missing, which was unusual. Although he frequently wandered off during the night, he was always back in bed by morning. Marianne had come downstairs, intending to find him.

She took one look at Sandra, covered in blood, and realized that whatever had happened to her, this was no time for questions. She grabbed the first thing to hand, a heavy tablecloth, wrapped it around her and steered her into one of the downstairs bathrooms. Then she called an ambulance.

By the time the paramedics arrived, Sandra had descended from screaming hysterics into catatonic silence. She was rigid and unresponsive. They established that she had no injuries, so they guessed the blood belonged to someone else. As she was unable or unwilling to tell them from whom it had come, and didn't need hospitalization, they called the police. As soon as Sergeant Parsloe discovered that the incident involved Richington Vale Winery, Sandra Richington-Blythe and a good deal of blood, he did a finger-tip pass to the MIT and Jack Dawes.

* * *

'Bloody hell, guv, not another corpse!' exclaimed Bugsy. 'I thought we'd already scored our hat-trick. Are we into extra time?'

Jack shook his head. 'No corpse yet, but I'm pretty sure one will turn up soon. Mrs Richington-Blythe arrived home early this morning, stark naked and covered in blood. Norman says they put her to bed, but her jaws are clamped shut with shock. They've called Doctor Griffin to her. I suggest we get out there and find out from him when she's likely to be fit to be questioned.'

When they got there, Sandra still hadn't said anything. Zack was at her bedside, but there was no sign of Jolyon, who was apparently away overnight at a meeting.

'Can we talk to her, Danny?' Bugsy asked.

The doctor was taking her blood pressure. 'You can try, Mike. She isn't in any immediate danger, but she's still badly traumatized. I can do some tests to see if the blood is hers, but there are no obvious injuries, unless she had a massive nosebleed, which is unlikely. And from the state of her feet, she's obviously run barefoot, over rough ground, for some distance.'

Bugsy frowned. 'In my book, there are only two reasons for taking all your clothes off — to have a shower or to have sex. It doesn't look like she had a shower.'

'I think we have two choices,' said Jack. 'Either we wait until she recovers enough to tell us what happened, or we get Uniform to search for a body.'

'Why don't we do both?' suggested Bugsy. 'We don't know if we're dealing with a body yet. There could be someone out there bleeding and in urgent need of help.'

They went into the hall where Sébastien and Marianne were waiting for news. 'Is she going to be all right?' asked Sébastien. 'Where did all that blood come from?'

'That's what we're here to find out, sir,' said Jack.

'It must be a stranger who broke in to rob us. Sandra confronted him and somehow he got cut.'

'Was she in the habit of carrying a knife, sir?' asked Bugsy.

'No, of course not. Now, if you'd said a broken vodka bottle . . .'

'She came in from outside,' offered Marianne, who so far hadn't spoken.

'How do mean, madam? Outside where?'

'She came in from the terrace, via the side door.'

'What was she doing out on the terrace at that time of the morning?' asked Sébastien, puzzled. 'You found her around seven thirty, didn't you, Mari? Sandra doesn't normally surface until noon, and only then for coffee and an illicit cigarette. What happened to her clothes? Did they have blood on them?'

'Seb, she wasn't wearing any,' said Marianne.

'My god! Are you saying she was out on the terrace, naked and covered in blood? Whatever had the woman been up to? I know she isn't "one of us", but all the same, I wouldn't have said she was unhinged . . .' He tailed off.

'May I ask where the other members of the family are?' asked Jack.

Sébastien replied. 'Father went to a meeting yesterday that ended late, so he stayed over at the hotel. Zack is in the bedroom with his mother. I imagine Robbie is already out in the vineyards, preparing for harvesting. He's our manager now. Marianne, what time did Robbie leave this morning?'

She looked at him anxiously. 'Seb, I don't know. I woke in the night and he wasn't lying beside me. I assumed he couldn't sleep and he'd gone for one of his walks, but when I woke this morning, he still wasn't there. I was about to go and look for him when Sandra staggered in.'

Jack and Bugsy exchanged glances. Just then, Dr Griffin came out of the bedroom with his case.

'Has she said anything, Danny?' asked Bugsy.

'Just two words: "He's dead." Then the sedative took effect and now she's asleep. She's likely to stay that way for several hours.'

Sébastien scowled. 'I'm going to ring Father. He needs to know about this.'

* * *

Jolyon was in the hotel restaurant ordering breakfast when his phone rang. 'What do you want, Sébastien? Surely you can cope for a couple of days without bothering me.' His companion reached under the table and squeezed his thigh. How much easier it was, he thought, to impress young women when away from home. He could tell them whatever he liked, and as long as he flashed the cash around, they believed him. Even better, he could forget all the troubles that were waiting for him back at the winery. What he didn't need was his son interrupting and reminding him.

'Father, this is important. You need to come home straight away. Sandra appeared, early this morning, naked and covered in someone else's blood. She's sedated and can't tell us what happened. The police are here — Dawes and the fat one — they're going to conduct a search for a body. I think you should be here, in case they find one.'

'Well, I don't. I've no idea what the stupid woman has been up to, but I've no intention of bailing her out. That goes for her half-witted son, too. I'll be home when I've completed my business here.' He terminated the call and ordered the full English. He needed to keep up his strength.

CHAPTER TWELVE

Uniformed officers searched the house from top to bottom, but found nothing leading to a blood-soaked corpse. Zack's bed hadn't been slept in. When asked where he'd spent the night, he said he'd slept in the back of his car. He'd been out, got home late, forgotten his keys and didn't want to disturb anyone. It was partly true, but he failed to mention Rosie had been in the car with him, for most of the evening.

They searched Richington Hall grounds, which were extensive. There was a walled rose garden, a lake with a fountain, even a maze, installed by Air Commodore Sir Donald Richington-Blythe, which was very complicated. It was 'Ducky's' idea of a joke to take tour visitors in there, abandon them in the centre and see how long it took them to find their way out. The first one to emerge won a bottle of wine. On one occasion, an elderly couple was lost in there overnight, and it had taken a great deal more than a bottle of wine to placate them. Bugsy reckoned the bloke must have had an unusual sense of humour. In any event, Sergeant Parsloe's officers had been told not to go in there. There was no route map, and he reasoned that it wouldn't help the search operation if all his coppers were blundering about behind hedges.

Once they'd conceded that there was no body in the immediate vicinity, there was only one obvious place left to search. The vineyard.

Jack reported this to Chief Superintendent Garwood, who was worried about what that would do to the manpower budget.

'Dawes, are you sure this is necessary? That vineyard is immense. It'll cost a fortune. Can't we wait until the blasted woman can tell us where the body is — that's if there is one?'

'We could, sir. But what if he's still alive?'

'Didn't she say, "He's dead"?'

'Would she necessarily know? It doesn't look like she hung about to take his pulse.'

Garwood was imagining the *Echo* headlines, if that turned out to be the case. *Police failed to search for wounded man due to budget constraints. Chief Superintendent George Garwood faces an inquiry into the death.* Could he risk that? It would scupper his next promotion. Added to which, he was hoping for election to Worshipful Master of his Masonic lodge. The owner of the vineyard was an influential member.

'All right, Dawes, but try to be as cost-effective as possible. And don't upset Jolyon Richington-Blythe.'

* * *

They started with the woods that flanked Richington Hall. They were very dense, with just a narrow track that wound steeply down to the vineyard, making searching even more difficult. Having established that the woods contained nothing more sinister than a decomposing fox, the team worked its way systematically across the rows of vines and down the hillside. Dogs had been given the scent and were barking excitedly.

Jack made it clear to the search party that they were not just looking for a dead or wounded man. 'We must be aware that although Mrs Richington-Blythe was found covered in someone else's blood, we mustn't assume she inflicted the injury.'

'What does that mean, sir?' asked a bright lad.

'It means, son, that there could still be someone else hiding out there in the vineyard with a knife or similar, and who isn't afraid to use it,' warned Bugsy. 'So watch yourselves, people.'

They were still searching at nightfall. Darkness descended on the vineyard very rapidly, so they had to deploy flashlights. Jack was wondering whether to call off the operation, but while there remained the possibility that someone needed to be rescued alive, he felt they must continue the search. Members of his MIT were out there, alongside the uniformed officers, although he had lost sight of them.

Bugsy was creeping in and out of the rows of vines, expecting at any moment to find a corpse, or worse, a lunatic with a machete. He felt a tap on his shoulder and jumped violently, heart pounding. He spun around, adrenalin pumping in readiness for a fight.

'Bloody hell, Taffy. Don't ambush me like that. I nearly had a heart attack.'

'Sorry, Sarge,' said Aled. 'I've found a trail of blood spatters. Not much, but it could be the path Mrs Richington-Blythe took when she ran home.'

'Yes, but ran home from where, son? That's what we need to find out. She was naked and covered in blood, but I doubt she was sprinting back from a catfight at the health spa.'

'I thought over there might be worth a look.' Aled shone his flashlight ahead until it picked up the old hut, tucked away in a corner of the vineyard that hadn't yet been explored.

'Well done, young Taffy. You might just be onto something.'

They blundered through the tangle of vines until they reached the door. There was a good deal of blood on the grass. Aled made to go inside but Bugsy held him back. He'd had a sudden flashback of a twenty-two-year-old detective constable, barely a month in the job, who had taken two bullets in the chest because Bugsy had failed to protect him.

He hadn't died, thank God, but it had been a lesson Bugsy would never forget. 'Not you, son. We don't know who's in there.'

Bracing himself, Bugsy kicked open the door and shouted. 'Police! Stay where you are.' It was pitch black inside, but the sickly, abattoir smell told him they'd found the body. The light from his flashlight told him it was the body of Robbie McKendrick.

* * *

By the crack of dawn next morning, the hut and surrounding vines had been cordoned off with police tape, and uniformed constables guarded the approach. They lifted the tape to allow the detectives to enter.

Jack patted Aled on the back. 'Well done, DC Williams. DCS Garwood will be pleased — mostly because you saved him the expense of searching the vineyard all the way down to the village.'

The SOCOs' vehicle was parked on the grass between the vines, next to the hut. The mortuary transport was parked behind it.

'I wonder what Gormless Gavin will make of this one, guv.' Bugsy spoke softly but not softly enough. The figure kneeling by Robbie's corpse responded without turning round.

'He won't make anything of it, Sergeant Malone, because he isn't here.'

It was all Bugsy could do not to cheer. Big Ron was back and irascible as ever, despite her sojourn in the sun. 'Good holiday, Doc?'

'Excellent, thank you. I hear you've been up to your old tricks, Inspector Dawes. I turn my back for a few weeks and you slaughter four unsuspecting members of the public. No chance of you releasing them for a funeral any time soon? Only we're getting a bit short of space down at the morgue. If you kill off any more, we shall have to start stacking them in a heap.' She scrambled to her feet, her protective suit sparing Bugsy the glimpse of sturdy knicker-leg. 'No mystery with this poor devil. Someone stuck a knife in his chest and he bled out.'

Jack was still conscious of the time it had taken to mount the search. 'Would he have survived, if we'd found him sooner, Doctor Hardacre?'

She shook her head. 'No chance. Losing this much blood, this fast, he'll have gone into haemorrhagic shock in seconds. Death will have followed minutes later. Unless you'd been on the spot when the knife went in, you couldn't have saved him, and even then, it would have been touch-and-go. I don't expect the post-mortem to throw up anything unusual, but I'll let you know. My guess would be that he'd had sex shortly before he died, and I expect to find a good deal of alcohol in his system, judging by those empty bottles.'

'Well, if you've gotta go, there are worse ways . . .' muttered Bugsy.

'Estimated time of death, Doctor?' asked Jack, knowing this time he'd get a sensible answer.

'Between four and eight yesterday morning is as close as I can get.' She held up a specimen envelope containing the knife. 'This may give us some clues, but don't hold your breath. Unless our killer left us a nice set of fingerprints, it's exactly like a thousand others in the vine-pruning business.' She turned to Bugsy. 'In case you're wondering, Sergeant, "Gormless Gavin" spoke highly of you, too.' She picked up her case and went out, indicating to the mortuary men that they could remove the body.

* * *

The next step was to inform the family. They were assembled in the Louis XVI drawing room, waiting for news, all except for Sandra, who was still heavily sedated. Suzy had joined them, more out of curiosity than to give moral support.

Jack broke the news as gently as he could. 'I'm sorry to have to tell you that we have found the body of Robbie McKendrick. He had been stabbed in the chest with a pruning knife.'

There were gasps of horror. Marianne Richington-Blythe went white and sat down, suddenly. For lack of any other female support, Suzy put an arm around her. Shocking though it was, there was worse to come.

Jolyon, who had decided to return home to the family, lest one of them said something ill-advised, went across to the drinks table and poured himself a treble malt whisky instead of wine. 'I gather my wife had something to do with this.' He took a long pull on the whisky. 'Did she find the body?'

'In a manner of speaking, sir.' Bugsy was treading carefully.

'Well, did she or didn't she? Spit it out, man.'

'I can see why she'd be covered in his blood,' said Sébastien, 'but why was she naked?'

'I can tell you why,' said Marianne, in barely more than a whisper. 'They were seeing each other for sex, weren't they? I've known Robbie has been with someone else for a while. He'd go off at night and come back in the morning, smelling of . . . her.'

'For goodness' sake, Marianne, why didn't you say something?' Jolyon was disgusted.

'Like what? "Oh, incidentally, Papa, I think your wife is having it off with my partner." What would you have done? Thrown them both out? Zack too? And I don't recall you mentioning anything about Sandra going missing at night.' This was a mite cruel, as everyone in the family knew that Jolyon and Sandra had separate bedrooms, and had done for years.

'Where did you find Robbie, Inspector?' asked Sébastien.

'In a hut, in the vineyard. We think Mrs Richington-Blythe had run from there when she arrived home.'

'Are you saying that my mother killed him?' Zack had entered the room, unheard, from a door behind them. They couldn't be sure how long he'd been listening, but he'd clearly heard the worst of it.

'We won't know that until she's well enough to be questioned, sir.' Bugsy felt sorry for the lad. Bad enough to have been dragged into this godawful family, without this.

He looked around at them with terrified eyes, like a cornered animal. 'My mother wouldn't kill anyone. I know you all think she's trash, but she isn't. The only bad thing she ever did was to marry you!' He hurled this at Jolyon, then ran from the room.

'Shall I go after him?' asked Suzy.

'No,' said Sébastien. 'Leave him to cool off. He's had a shock.'

'What happens now, Inspector?' asked Jolyon.

'We wait for Mrs Richington-Blythe to recover, then we ask her what happened,' replied Jack. 'Our forensics team are examining the location and the weapon, which will hopefully give us some answers. Would you like me to assign a family liaison officer, to keep you up to date with developments?'

'Definitely not!' Jolyon was adamant. 'We don't want any more people gossiping and prying into our private affairs.'

'I'm afraid we shall have to leave an officer outside Mrs Richington-Blythe's room, sir,' said Bugsy.

'What the blazes for? I'll inform you when she says anything sensible.'

I bet you will, thought Bugsy, *and you'll make sure she doesn't say anything, until after you've approved it*. 'All the same, sir, it's police procedure in the case of a witness to a murder.'

Jolyon made a noise that sounded like a snort and turned his back on them.

* * *

By the time Zack reached the Blythe Spirit, he was choking with anger. Everyone in the pub reacted. Rosie hurried from behind the bar and put her arms around him. Matt could see Zack was in a bad way and poured him a stiff drink. Sheila and Miles were sitting at a table nearby, having called in for some food after church choir practice. They got up and came across to see if they could help.

'What is it, mate?' asked Miles. 'What's happened?'

'Robbie's dead. They're saying my mother killed him,' he spluttered.

'Who are?' asked Rosie.

'The police.'

'That can't be right, surely. I saw Robbie only a couple of days ago, walking past the shop,' said Sheila. 'He can't be dead.'

'The family believes she did it, too,' said Zack.

'But why would she?' asked Rosie, baffled. 'Was it some kind of accident? How did it happen?'

Village folk abandoned their drinks and were gathering around, keen to hear more. 'Freddy and I saw some police activity from a distance, in the vineyard this morning,' said Matt. 'We just assumed there'd been some kind of accident with the harvesting equipment.'

Someone joined in the gruesome speculation. 'You hear of workers, busy at the end of a row, slipping under the wheels of a tractor when it backs out.'

'I even heard of a case where someone caught a piece of clothing in an automatic harvester and got pulled in,' added someone else, not to be outdone.

'Is that what happened, Zack, lad?'

'I don't know,' sobbed Zack. 'All I know is that my mother didn't do it.'

'You can't go back home in this state,' said Matt. 'You'd better stay here in the pub. We don't have any guests at the moment.' He turned to Rosie. 'Sort a room for him, please. Freddy will cook him a meal. We need to get some food inside him. He looks terrible.'

CHAPTER THIRTEEN

While Zack was eating hotpot in the pub, Jolyon, Sébastien and Marianne were sitting around the vast dining table in Richington Hall, silently pretending to eat, but just pushing the food around their plates. Sandra remained heavily sedated. The elephant in the room overwhelmed all else. Now there had been three murders directly connected to the Richington Vale vineyard. The death of Patricia Chambers — although ostensibly unrelated — had taken place in the events suite, so she could be considered a fourth. The police didn't appear to be making any headway with finding the culprits.

Sébastien broke the silence. 'Father, do you think the time has come to tell the police about the anonymous letter?'

'Definitely not!' Jolyon gave up the pretence of eating and slammed down his knife and fork. 'What would be the point? It's the work of some crackpot, jealous of our situation.'

'What situation would that be, Papa?' asked Marianne innocently. 'We're a dysfunctional family, struggling to run an ailing business behind a pathetic facade of wealth and respectability. Who in their right mind would be jealous of that?'

Sébastien continued. 'I don't think the writer was a crackpot, Father. The message was a quotation, most likely biblical.' He went across to the antique French sideboard, pulled open a drawer and extracted an envelope.

Jolyon scowled. 'I thought I told you to destroy that, Marianne.'

'You did, Papa. I decided not to.'

Sébastien read out the single sentence. '*Whoever is greedy for unjust gain, troubles his own household.* It's a direct threat to the family, Father. Someone is accusing you and the company of making money at the expense of the workers. I think we should hand the letter over to Inspector Dawes and see what he makes of it.'

'So do I,' agreed Marianne. 'It would be irresponsible not to.'

'No! I forbid it!' Jolyon's colour and blood pressure were rising with temper, as they always did when he didn't get his own way.

'Sorry, Father, but this time, you've been outvoted.'

* * *

When Sébastien and Marianne turned up asking to speak to Inspector Dawes, the desk sergeant showed them straight into the interview room and telephoned through to the MIT.

'What? Both of 'em?' asked Bugsy. 'All right, I'll tell him.'

He found Jack looking at the rapidly increasing number of notes and photos on the whiteboard and wondering what he was missing.

'I wonder what they want, guv?'

'Let's go and find out. Jolyon isn't with them, so it's either something he doesn't know about or he disapproves.'

The anonymous letter was something of a surprise.

'We've written the date Papa received it on the envelope,' said Marianne, helpfully.

Oh good, thought Bugsy. *That means they've all handled it, and we don't stand a snowball's of finding the sender's prints among all the other smudges. That's if there were any to find in the first place.*

Jack handled it between finger and thumb, by the extreme corners, and placed it in a transparent evidence envelope. You never knew — Forensics might be able to salvage something. He read the sentence aloud, so that Bugsy could hear. *'Whoever is greedy for unjust gain, troubles his own household.'*

'What do you think it means, Inspector?' asked Sébastien.

'More to the point, sir, what do you and your father think it means?' asked Jack.

Sébastien and Marianne exchanged glances. 'Father thinks it's a jealous crackpot with a grudge. Marianne and I think it was written by someone who believes — mistakenly, I should add — that Father is guilty of agricultural malpractice. We see it as a veiled threat to our family, which is why we have brought it to you.'

'And it arrived the day before Mr McKendrick was killed?' asked Bugsy. He was surprised Marianne didn't seem overly upset, but then, would you grieve for a partner who'd been knocking off your stepmother? Probably not.

Sébastien nodded. 'I don't think any of us seriously believes that Sandra was responsible. She was clearly in the wrong place at the wrong time, and certainly doing the wrong thing, but that doesn't make her a murderer.'

Bugsy remembered what Danny — Dr Griffin — had said about Richington-Blythe evading his ethical responsibilities, supported by the crooked Dr Anstruther. But would someone commit murder simply because they didn't like the way the boss operated? Surely they'd just blow the whistle.

Jack was thinking along the same lines. Murder was a rather drastic response to an accusation of negligence. 'Thank you for coming in. Leave it with us, we'll make some enquiries.'

As they left, Bugsy said, 'Mind how you go,' more for something less feeble to say than 'Cheerio' than a genuine belief that they were in danger.

* * *

Before he passed the letter to Forensics, Aled photocopied it and pinned it to the whiteboard, beneath the photo of Robbie McKendrick. The team studied it.

'What next, sir?' Gemma asked.

Jack wondered if any of the other victims had received an anonymous letter before they were killed. It was a long shot, but worth asking. 'Gemma, contact Constable Wainwright — she's Barbara Beacham's FLO. Ask her to visit Mrs Beacham, ostensibly to update her, and enquire whether Bob Beacham received any strange letters before he died. Aled, you do the same with Godzilla — I mean, Miss Latimer — at Doctor Anstruther's surgery. Find out if he'd had any unusual notes, just prior to the FATACC.'

Aled flinched. 'Can't Gemma visit Godzilla, sir, and I'll contact Fiona? I don't think Miss Latimer likes me.'

'You need to grow a pair, lad,' said Bugsy.

'That's just it, Sarge. Whenever I see Godzilla, it reminds me of all those embarrassing questions she asked about the pair I already have.'

Jack picked up his jacket. 'Obviously McKendrick didn't receive one, or Marianne would have handed it over. That just leaves Patricia Chambers. Corrie said she lived alone. Bugsy, you and I will take a look around her cottage.'

* * *

PC Wainwright pulled up outside the Beachams' cottage. Barbara saw her coming and opened the front door. 'Have you caught him? Do you know who killed my Bob? When can I have his body for a proper funeral?'

They went inside. 'Not yet, Mrs Beacham, but the Murder Investigation Team is following every possible line of enquiry.'

They made tea and Barbara produced a cake. 'Battenberg — it's my Bob's favourite.' Her eyes filled with tears. 'It *was* his favourite, I should say.'

Fiona began gently, 'Can you remember, Mrs Beacham, whether Bob received any odd letters before he died?'

'No, nothing like that. I'd have remembered. I mean, people don't write letters anymore, do they? They send emails and private messages.' She thought about it. 'Hang on a minute. There might have been something . . .'

'It would help if you could remember.'

'When they gave me back Bob's overalls, you know, the ones he was wearing when it happened . . .'

'Yes?'

'I haven't had the heart to wash them, yet. I will get around to it, but not yet.'

'No, of course not.'

'There was an envelope sticking out of one of the pockets. I assumed it was a note with instructions, left for him by Mr Richington-Blythe. He did that sometimes, if he couldn't reach him on his phone.'

'Do you still have it, Barbara?'

'I expect so. Do you want me to look?'

'Yes, please.'

They went into the utility room, where a laundry basket was overflowing with Bob's washing, which Barbara hadn't been able to face. She fished out the overalls and went to pull out the envelope that was still sticking out of the pocket. Fiona stopped her.

'No, don't touch it, Barbara. Let me.' Fiona extracted a plastic wallet from her pocket and carefully slipped in the envelope by its edges. 'I'll take it back to Inspector Dawes. I'll let you know if it's anything important. Now, is there another piece of Battenberg going?'

* * *

DC Williams pushed open the door to the surgery and advanced, cautiously, to reception, where Miss Latimer was giving some hopeful patient the third degree. Aled waited until she had dismissed the poor chap with a curt, 'Nonsense. Take a couple of paracetamols and lie down. You'll be fine.' Reluctantly, the man turned away, unsure quite what had just happened, but wondering how that advice would cure his embarrassing rash. Aled approached.

Godzilla glared. 'And what exactly do you think is wrong with you?'

'Oh, nothing, Miss Latimer. Nothing at all. I'm DC Williams from the Murder Investigation Team.' He produced his warrant card. She took it, pulled her glasses down from where they were perched on top of her head and examined it minutely. Then, still suspicious, she handed it back. 'What do you want? I gave you all the information I had last time. That technical chap copied it all from the computer.'

'I need to know whether Doctor Anstruther received any strange letters before he was killed.'

Aled had unwittingly lighted the blue touchpaper of this particular firework, and unfortunately for him, he was unable to retire immediately. Miss Latimer went a very unhealthy colour and for some moments appeared unable to speak. Then she went off like a supersonic rocket. 'Yes, he did! It was libellous, vicious and a wicked calumny!'

'May I see it, please?'

'No, you may not, young man, for the simple reason that I shredded it. I didn't want the doctor to be upset by it.'

'That's a pity, because it might have helped us to find the person who ran him over. Perhaps you remember what it said?'

Aled reckoned her voice rose by enough decibels to register on Heathrow's jet traffic control. 'I'll never forget it. How anybody could write something so vile, about a wonderful man like Doctor Anstruther, I just don't know. As you're a police officer, I'll write it down for you, but if it ends up on the front page of the *Echo*, I'll know where it came from.' She scribbled it on a notepad, tore it off, folded it in half and handed it over. Aled took it and beat a hasty retreat. As he left, he passed the man with the rash, on his way back in to try again.

'I'd leave it five minutes, if I were you, mate.'

* * *

Jack and Bugsy searched Patricia Chambers' cottage but found no anonymous letter. She had a number of photographs on her piano — nephews and nieces, a cat, long dead, and a picture of the school where she had taught for so many years. She was sitting, knees modestly together, in the centre of a group photograph of the entire school.

Bugsy picked it up. 'I remember those panoramic school photos. If you were nippy, you could get in it twice. You stood at one end, then when the camera started to roll, you ran like stink behind the other kids and got pictured at the other end as well.' He paused. 'She was a nice old dear. It says at the bottom, "Richington Vale Primary School. Headmistress Miss Patricia Chambers BTh." What does that mean?'

'It means she had a Bachelor of Theology degree,' said Jack. 'Interesting.'

'She was a fully licensed God-botherer. Why would anyone want to bump her off?'

'That's what we're here to try and find out. I believe it wasn't so much about what she was as what she knew.' Jack studied the school photo. 'Do any of those children look at all familiar to you? The two coppernobs, sitting together on the right?'

'No, guv. All kids look the same to me. Pesky, smelly, festering heaps of infection, the lot of 'em. They get under your feet when they're little and under your skin when they're adolescents, nicking cars, dealing drugs and calling you a "pig".' He pulled something from the bookcase. 'Hey, Jack, what about this? This might tell us something. It's her journal.'

'Well spotted, Bugsy. We'll take it away and ask Gemma to read through it.'

* * *

Back at the station, they put together the anonymous letters and pinned the copies to the whiteboard. Gemma stood in front to explain to the team. 'They're all quotes from the Bible.' She pointed to Jolyon's. '*Whoever is greedy for unjust gain, troubles his own household*. That's Proverbs 15:27. In basic English that means, "Make a profit dishonestly and you get your family into trouble." The one Bob Beacham received, *The wages of sin is death*, that's Romans 6:23. It's pretty much self-explanatory. Someone believes Beacham took money for something crooked, and now he's dead. Doctor Anstruther's needs no translation. *Ye are a forger of lies. Ye are a physician of no value.* Job 13:4. I'm guessing that refers to his corrupt habit of making sure that if any of the workers had an accident or contracted a disease, it would always be recorded as their own fault, due to their own negligence, or a disregard for health and safety rules. The company would never be held responsible. Whoever wrote these got it right on the money, in my opinion.' She sat down.

'Thanks, Gemma. I had no idea you knew so much about the Bible.' Jack was impressed.

'I don't, sir. I'm an atheist. I just googled it.'

Bugsy rolled his eyes. 'Almighty Google — god of the internet.'

'What I can't work out,' said Aled, 'if they each got a letter and then died, why didn't Potty Chambers and Robbie McKendrick get one?'

'I think the ones who got letters were killed because of what they'd done,' said Jack. 'Miss Chambers and McKendrick were killed for what they knew. And I think it was spur-of-the-moment, not premeditated, like the others.'

'Jolyon Richington-Blythe got a letter and he's still alive,' said DC Mitchell.

'Indeed he is, Mitch. But we don't know how long after they received their letter that the others were killed. I'd suggest putting an officer to guard him, but he'd never allow it. The best we can do is to advise him to be cautious.'

'Do you really think his life's in danger, sir?' asked Aled.

'Yes, I do. Maybe not immediately, but I believe someone is planning it — and slowly, to inflict the most suffering.'

CHAPTER FOURTEEN

Sheila breathed in the intoxicating fragrance of late-summer flowers and the earthy smell of chrysanthemums, dewy-fresh from Miles's market garden that morning. The Flower Pot, like all florists, was a cool sanctuary on an oppressive day. She never tired of it. It provided the stability and security she had needed for so long. Soon, the healing process would be complete.

'Any chance of a coffee?' Miles came in via the back door, carrying another armful of blooms.

Sheila poured one from the machine that supplied coffee for customers who needed time to choose their flowers — mostly impending brides and their mothers. A good deal of custom came from weddings and funerals. She was aware of the four bodies in the morgue, awaiting a funeral, when the police saw fit to release them. Then there was Christmas, Valentine's Day and Mother's Day. All in all, the Flower Pot did well for a village florist, and it was one of the few businesses in Richington Vale that wasn't owned by the Richington-Blythes.

Sheila and Miles shared the same fair complexion and hair the colour of autumn leaves. They were unmistakeably brother and sister. Although only three years older than

Miles, Sheila tended to take the lead in any important decisions. It had been she who had decided they should start up the market garden business in Richington Vale. Neither had a soulmate, and both had given up hope of finding one. The propagation and sale of plants had evolved from their faith. As youngsters, they'd had little time for religion, nor the phoney snake oil merchants who peddled it. Back then, it had been hard to see the love of any god in their lives. But as they matured, they saw God in the plants and flowers they produced, and their faith was a comfort and an inspiration.

'Miles, you don't regret coming back to Richington Vale, do you?'

'Course not, sis. It was the right decision. The only way to lay our ghosts, once and for all. And we've nearly done it, haven't we?'

'Yes, we have. Very soon, all those bad memories, the deprivation and injustice will be behind us.'

* * *

Gemma had been trawling through Miss Chambers' journal, looking for something, anything, that might provide a clue to her killer. Mostly, it was stuff about the church, jumble sales and coffee mornings in aid of various causes. The most important one for Miss Chambers at the time of her death appeared to be raising funds for the vicar's latest project, the restoration of the derelict Richington Vale children's home, to convert it into a boxing club.

Finally, among all the village news, she came upon an entry that she thought might be significant and showed it to Bugsy.

I saw him again, today. I could be completely mistaken but I don't think so, despite my ever-worsening memory for faces. (Senility and dementia, like Scylla and Charybdis, lie in wait to devour me.) Although he is cheerful enough in public, I have caught him looking troubled and angry when he believes nobody can see him, and why wouldn't he? I wish I could think of a way to help him, but I know he

*would resent any intrusion into the protective shell he has built around
himself. I fear he has done, or is about to do, something wicked. I may
have to share my fears with that nice Sergeant Parsloe.*

'Who do you think she meant, Sarge?'

Bugsy scratched his head. 'Bugger only knows. It could
be any number of blokes in the village — Zack, Sébastien, the
two chaps from the pub, Miles what's-his-name who runs the
market garden, and McKendrick was still alive when she wrote
that. Not Jolyon, he isn't cheerful, even in public. Could even
be the vicar. He has a smile for everybody — mostly because he
doesn't know what they're up to. Your guess is as good as mine.'

Jack's reaction was very similar. 'Good work, Gemma. It's
a pity Miss Chambers didn't have time to speak to Norman
before it was too late.'

* * *

'Corrie, what do you know about Patricia Chambers?' Jack
was eating pizza with six different toppings — one of his
favourites, but a rare treat, as Corrie didn't consider it 'proper
food' for a chef's husband.

'Nothing, really. Only that she seems to have taught
everyone in Richington Vale over the age of about fifteen,
except the posh ones, who went to private schools. And she
was a fierce fundraiser. Certainly nothing that would incite
anyone to poison her.'

'That's what I thought,' said Jack. 'And in any case, if
she'd upset you at school, you wouldn't wait for ten years
after she'd retired to get your own back, would you?'

'No. You'd put frogs in her desk or throw darts at the
blackboard, while she was writing on it.'

'Is that what you did?' asked Jack, amused.

'No. Cynthia did — but I got the blame.'

He chewed thoughtfully. 'Bugsy says Doctor Griffin
thinks Sandra Richington-Blythe will be well enough to be
interviewed tomorrow.'

Corrie pulled a face. 'Good luck with that.'

'I'm surprised Jolyon didn't throw her out when he found out what she'd been up to with McKendrick.' Jack poured himself a glass of wine.

'If I'd been her, I'd have walked out years ago. He's ghastly, and rumour has it he doesn't have the money to support her lifestyle any longer, so why stay? Rosie from the Blythe Spirit told Carlene that Zack's already left. The lads at the pub are putting him up until he can find somewhere for him and Rosie to live.'

'That means there are only four of them in that great big house now. They must be rattling around.'

'Maybe Suzy, the Wine Woman, will move in. She's renting a cottage in the village at present — although, according to Carlene, she doesn't take any part in village life. There's another rumour that she and Sébastien are an item.'

'The amount of gossiping you and Carlene do, I wonder you find time to cook.'

'We work in a scandal-rich industry, sweetheart. You'd be surprised what folk let slip when you're serving food. It's almost as if you're invisible.'

'Any more grist from the culinary rumour mill?'

'Just that they're saying it was McKendrick who broke into Leggett, Leggett and Fallover and bashed Peter Leggett over the head. Apparently, he let it slip in the pub when he was rat-arsed. McKendrick, I mean, not the solicitor.'

'Try not to be so lurid, darling. Did he say why he broke in, when he was . . . er . . . tired and emotional?'

'Yep. If Bugsy were here, he'd say "Follow the money." Sandra told McKendrick she was going to divorce Jolyon and bolt with as much of his cash as she could. He wanted to see how much, if any, was in Marianne's name and if she'd made a will in his favour, but he couldn't get into the computer. No point now. He can't spend it where he's gone.'

'Very true. No pockets in a shroud.'

'Now I've finished being your snitch, have you left me any wine in that bottle, or shall I open another one?'

* * *

They went to interview Sandra the following morning. Considering her ordeal, she was remarkably chipper.

'We weren't sure you'd still be here, madam . . . er . . . Mrs Richington-Blythe,' Bugsy began.

'Oh, for Christ's sake, call me Sandra. Too bloody right I'm still here. My solicitor told me not to leave the marital home under any circumstances, until an agreement about money had been reached. So here I am, and here I'm going to stay, until the mean old bastard coughs up.'

'Your marital arrangements are your own business,' said Jack. 'We're here to ask you what you know about the death of Robbie McKendrick.'

'There isn't much to know. We'd gone down to the hut for a bit of how's-your-father, drank a lot and shagged each other senseless, then fell asleep. I woke up next morning and found him lying there, with a pruning knife in his chest. And there *I* was — covered in his blood. Well, as you can imagine, I freaked. I just ran back here and passed out. When I woke up, that nice Doctor Griffin was standing over me. That's it, really.'

'Did you see anybody else hanging about?' asked Bugsy.

'Sweetheart, if the vicar had been standing there in just his dog collar, I wouldn't have noticed. I was scared shitless.' She paused, suddenly suspicious. 'Here — you don't think I did it, do you? I'm telling you now, I bloody well didn't!'

'Calm down, Sandra. We're just following all lines of enquiry, that's all,' said Bugsy.

'Well, you can stop following that one, straight away. He was alive when I fell asleep and dead when I woke up.'

'What does Marianne say about all this?' Jack was thinking that the atmosphere in the house must be even frostier than it had been before.

'Well, she isn't thrilled, obviously. But they'd been on the point of splitting up, anyway. I guess I just hurried things along. Is that all? Only I could do with a coffee and a fag.'

They left a uniformed constable to take her statement.

* * *

When George Garwood's private line rang, he thought it was Cynthia. It wasn't. It was Jolyon Richington-Blythe and he wasn't happy.

'Gee-Gee? Jolyon here. I need some of your men to put a watch on my vineyard for a few days.'

Garwood thought he'd better tread carefully. And he wished Jolyon wouldn't call him Gee-Gee. It was a stupid nickname from his prep school days that had stuck. The surveillance that Jolyon wanted would take considerable budget, but he needed his lodge vote if he was ever going to become Worshipful Master. What he didn't need was a complaint to his senior officer and Jolyon's golf buddy, Commander Sir Barnaby Featherstonehaugh, that he wasn't using police resources to protect the public and their property.

'Hello, Jolyon. Why do you need surveillance? What's the problem?'

'Someone is setting out to ruin me. You'll already know about the murders of my manager and my doctor. Then some old girl dies during an event in the winery, and now my replacement manager has been killed.'

'I have my best man on the cases, Jolyon. Inspector Dawes and his team are investigating every avenue.'

'I dare say, but that's not the worst of it — my vines are being systematically poisoned during the night. I've got ten acres, brown and shrivelled, just as harvesting has started. And to cap it all, I received another of those damn silly notes this morning. It said, *An inheritance gained hastily in the beginning, will not be blessed in the end.* What the blazes is that supposed to mean?'

'I've no idea, Jolyon, but I'll get my people onto it. Who do you think is poisoning your vines?'

'I know who's at the back of it — it's Sandra. That's who it is! The bloody woman is out to finish me, any way she can. I should never have got involved with her in the first place.'

George and several other cronies had long been curious about that. Sandra was so different from Jolyon's first wife,

Dominique. 'Why did you marry her? Your friends have often wondered.'

'It's a long story, Gee-Gee. What are you going to do about my dying vines? The thing is, I have a big event coming up. Representatives from a huge French wine consortium are coming over to stay at Richington Hall, and I'm going to showcase my sparkling Chardonnay. If I can get them to invest heavily, I'm saved. Can't you get that Dawes fellow to look into it? He seems to have more sense than the average copper.'

'Not really, Jolyon. Dawes is head of the Murder Investigation Team. He's already looking into the four bodies that have turned up in and around the winery.'

'But this *is* murder. The blasted woman is murdering my vines — and my reputation. Although I don't believe she's behind the anonymous letters. She can barely write a shopping list, let alone a quotation.'

Garwood did a rapid cost–benefit analysis and decided it wouldn't hurt to throw some human resources at the problem. 'OK, Jolyon, we'll stake out your vineyard for few nights, and I'll put a tail on Sandra. How about that?'

'Good. And you'll arrest the bitch?'

'If we catch her breaking the law, even if it's only criminal damage, we'll take her into custody.'

CHAPTER FIFTEEN

'Really, sir?' Jack was amazed that Garwood had agreed to the surveillance, even under the Old Pals' Act. 'It will eat into the manpower budget, and it's already a bit lean.'

'I'm not talking about a full-scale operation like the one we deployed to find McKendrick's body. Just a few officers for a couple of nights. Enough to satisfy Richington-Blythe.'

'I'll assign DC Mitchell to Sandra Richington-Blythe.' Mitch had the ability to blend in with the scenery when it came to tailing someone.

'As you wish, Dawes. Keep me informed.' Garwood picked up his phone. This was the signal that he'd been dismissed, so Jack left Garwood's office and went back to the incident room, where there had been something of a breakthrough.

Aled was keen to tell him. 'Sir, do you remember me mentioning the Evidence and Biometric Identity Management department?'

'I do. Have they come up with something useful?'

'Yes and no, sir. There's good news and bad news.'

'Give me the good news. I can do with some.'

'On re-examining Miss Chambers' flask, they found an eyelash, stuck in the screw cap. It doesn't belong to Miss Chambers, because it's ginger with traces of brown mascara.'

'So a red-haired woman, wearing make-up, pinched Miss Chambers' flask when she wasn't looking, emptied in the cyanide, blinked, screwed the cap back on and slipped it back in her bag.' It was a convenient conclusion, so Jack jumped to it.

'Careful, sir,' warned Gemma. 'Your presumptions are showing.'

'That's right, guv,' agreed Bugsy. 'It could be a ginger-haired bloke who wears mascara.'

'Like who?' challenged Jack.

'Gormless Gavin for a start, when he's on stage performing. Not that I'm suggesting he poisoned Potty Chambers. I'm just saying it isn't impossible for it to be a bloke — that's all.'

'What's the bad news?' Jack could just glimpse the end of his tether, disappearing into the distance.

'The bad news is that the lash didn't have the follicle attached, so it won't give us the DNA of the killer. The Biometrics Department says scientists in the US think they've found a way of extracting DNA from follicle-less hairs, but it's early days and their findings wouldn't stand up in court.'

'That, young Taffy,' remarked Bugsy, 'is the most unhelpful voyage of discovery since Raleigh cycled back from America with his saddlebag full of fags and chips. Haven't we got anything more substantial?'

'We know the poison was put in the flask *after* Miss Chambers got to the venue. It might help if we knew how many ginger-haired people were at the event,' suggested Gemma. 'Nearly everyone had left by the time we got there.'

'I'll phone Mrs Dawes. She's very observant and has an excellent memory. She was catering there throughout the day.'

If Corrie thought it a weird question, she didn't say so. Jack would have his reasons. 'Well, there was Rosie, the barmaid from the pub, helping to serve the drinks. Then there were the Bartons, Sheila and Miles from the Flower Pot. They were in charge of the Dionysus display. Suzy Black, the Wine Woman, was there, obviously, although her hair is more auburn. I think Sandra Richington-Blythe is a redhead.

She has it dyed blonde, but her roots were showing. And of course, the editor of the *Echo* is gingery. Oh yes, and Matt from the pub popped in, to see if we needed more glasses — he loaned them for nothing, which was kind. His partner, Freddy, has put blonde highlights in his ginger hair. It looked really nice. I'm thinking of asking him to do mine.'

'Corrie, concentrate. Is that all of them?' asked Jack.

'It's all the ones I can identify. There were upwards of sixty people there. Some of them will have had ginger hair, by the law of averages.'

He sighed. 'Yes, of course they will.'

'I could ask Cynthia for the guest list, but it won't tell you what colour hair they had. And I believe there were some gatecrashers, so it won't be comprehensive, either.'

Jack sighed again. Bereft of a paddle, he was drifting irretrievably up the proverbial creek. 'Thank you, darling. See you tonight. Don't bother cooking for me, I'll be late. We're staking out the vineyard to try and catch whoever's poisoning the vines.'

'I saw the dead ones though the window when I was there. Such a shame. There was something peculiar about the formation of the brown lines. I'll let you know when I remember it.'

* * *

Aled and Gemma volunteered to join the officers skulking about in the darkened vineyard, mainly for the overtime. Jack and Bugsy hung about for a while but reckoned they looked a bit conspicuous, so they decided to have supper in the Blythe Spirit. They'd still be close enough to be on call if the troops detained anyone.

Matt welcomed them with his sunny smile. 'Good evening, officers. To what do we owe the pleasure?'

'Some colleagues are checking security in the Richington-Blythe vineyard, so we thought we'd pop in for a couple of pints and some grub, and stay out of their way,' said Bugsy.

'My wife says the hotpot here's very popular,' said Jack. 'She's planning to come and ask your chef for the recipe.'

'He'd be delighted, wouldn't you, Freddy?'

Freddy had come through from the kitchen to see if anyone wanted to order. 'I'd be honoured, officer. Coriander's Cuisine is culinary legend around these parts and beyond. Will that be two hotpots for your good selves?'

'And two more over here, please Freddy.' Sheila and Miles had called in, after a meeting at the vicarage to plan the Harvest Festival celebrations. Their contributions in the form of fruit and flower arrangements were much admired. 'What's the operation this time, Inspector?' asked Sheila. 'I hope you're not looking for another body. It was terrible, what happened to Mr McKendrick.'

Miles admonished her. 'You shouldn't ask, Sheila. It might be top secret.'

'No, sir, just routine security checks. Nothing to worry about.' Jack was tilting at fate — that imaginary foe that preordains outcomes. Fate tilted right back.

* * *

Aled and Gemma had split up, to cover as much ground as possible. They started from opposite sides, at the top of the hill, close to the woods that flanked Richington Hall, and worked their way slowly down towards the village.

It was tricky going. They had been told not to use torches, as this was meant to be a covert surveillance, so there were plenty of opportunities to trip over roots and bump into fences. Aled lost his way several times. To him, one row of vines looked much like another, even in daylight, never mind in the dark. Gemma had brought a thermos, and paused at a convenient spot for a coffee. She had hardly unscrewed the lid when she heard it.

It was some distance away, but the sound carried on the still night air. It was unmistakeable. Somewhere, a woman was screaming. On the opposite side, Aled heard it too, as did the uniformed constables working across the vineyard.

The Blythe Spirit was virtually empty when the screaming started. Freddy was cleaning his cooker and Matt was down in the cellar, preparing ale for the next day. Rosie had finished work for the night and gone home to wash her hair. Zack had driven into Kings Richington. Apart from Jack and Bugsy, only Dave remained. Bugsy had bought him a pint when last orders were called, and he was wondering if he could finish it and wangle another before 'time'. No chance now.

At the first scream, Bugsy and Jack exchanged glances, then dashed outside.

The sound was coming from the garden of a cottage some hundred yards from the pub. The workers' cottages in the main street were terraced — this one was end-of-terrace and rather larger. Like the others, it belonged to the Richington Vale Winery and was rented out. By his own admission, Bugsy was built for comfort rather than speed, so Jack got to the scene first, but it had been a sprint finish.

It was pitch black, no street lights, and the cottage was in darkness. In the light of his torch, Jack saw a woman lying face down on the square patch of grass that passed for a front garden. His first thought was that it was Sandra. Jolyon had told Garwood that he suspected her of poisoning his vines out of spite. What if he had caught and attacked her?

Jack gently lifted her up. It wasn't Sandra — it was Suzy Black, the Master of Wine.

She was conscious, but her face was covered in blood from a split lip, and from the state of her eye, Jack reckoned it would be closed and black by morning. He helped her to her feet, and she winced as he took her arm. Bugsy eased the bunch of keys from her grasp, and eventually found one that unlocked the front door. Seconds later, Gemma arrived, followed by the uniformed constables.

'I'll call an ambulance,' said Gemma.

'No, please,' Suzy whispered painfully through the split lip. 'No ambulance.'

'You could have broken ribs, miss,' said Bugsy.

'I know, but poor Jolyon has had such a lot of bad luck. I don't want to add to his troubles.'

'Who did this to you?' asked Bugsy.

'I've no idea.'

'We really should get someone to look at you,' said Jack.

'I'll phone Danny,' offered Bugsy.

'That's Doctor Griffin,' explained Jack. 'Are you OK with that?'

She nodded.

While Gemma helped Suzy into bed, Bugsy went outside to stand down the uniformed constables. No point carrying on with the surveillance now their cover had been blown. The whole village was alert, with cottage lights on all down the main street. People had come out and were standing on their doorsteps, trying to see what was going on.

He went back inside, where Gemma was making tea. 'Where's young Taffy?'

She handed Bugsy a mug. 'No idea, Sarge, we were working opposite sides of the vineyard.'

Seconds later, Aled burst in, his nose bleeding profusely.

'What happened to you?' asked Bugsy. 'Did someone attack you?'

Aled looked shamefaced. 'No, Sarge. I was running and fell over a vine root in the dark and bashed my nose. I think it's broken.'

'Well, don't stand there bleeding all over Miss Black's rug. That's Danny — Doctor Griffin — pulling up outside. I'll get him to look at you after he's seen to Miss Black.'

Thirty minutes later, Dr Griffin was able to declare that Miss Black's injuries were painful but not as bad as they might appear, and Aled's nose was badly bent out of shape but not broken.

'Miss Black doesn't have any broken bones or internal injuries. It could have been much worse. Richington Vale is turning into the village of the damned, when a young woman can't let herself into her house at night without being attacked. You will catch whoever did this, Mike?' He made it sound more of an assumption than a question.

Bugsy nodded. 'We'll catch him, Danny, don't you worry.'

CHAPTER SIXTEEN

Jack decided to leave questioning Suzy Black until the next day. Her split lip made it painful for her to speak, and according to Dr Griffin she needed to sleep. Next morning, when Jack and Bugsy arrived at her cottage, Sébastien let them in. He'd brought a huge bouquet of flowers from the Flower Pot and was comforting her. As it turned out, there was little she could tell them.

'You won't upset her, will you, officers? She's had a terrible ordeal.'

'It's all right, Seb. I'm fine now. The police need to know what happened, in case the attacker targets someone else.' She fixed her gaze on Jack. 'I'd been working late up at the winery. Jolyon has a big presentation planned, and my job will be to extol the virtues of the Richington Vale sparkling Chardonnay, which is the jewel in the crown of his brand. When I got home, I parked the car as usual and I was walking up the path to the house, when someone in black leaped out at me. He must have been hiding in the shadows in my garden. He snatched my bag, then tried to grab my keys to the winery. I screamed and hung on, so he knocked me down, and I think he must have kicked me in the face. He ran off when you all came to my rescue. Seb thinks he wanted my keys so he could get in and damage the winery, but who would do that?'

'Can you describe your attacker, miss?'

'Not really. He was tall-ish, but not as tall as you, Inspector, and well-built, but not as solid as the sergeant. That's about it. It was dark and he was all in black. Even his face was covered. It happened very fast.'

Jack remembered what Garwood had told him about Jolyon suspecting Sandra was behind the attempts to sabotage the vineyard and ruin him. 'Could it have been a woman?'

Suzy thought about this. 'I guess it could have been. But who? And why?'

Those were the questions that Jack would like answered.

'I'm making arrangements for Suzy to move into Richington Hall,' said Sébastien. 'She can't stay here. It isn't safe.'

Remembering what it had been like on his last visit to the Hall, Bugsy wondered if, indeed, she would be any safer there. It certainly wasn't any more cheerful.

* * *

George Garwood was sitting in his office, arranging his new pens in perfect formation on the pen-rest, as though they were about to take off for a maiden flight. He adjusted his in-tray so that it sat directly parallel to his out-tray, then — horror of horrors — he spotted a greasy finger mark on the highly polished surface of his mahogany desk. That would be Sergeant Malone's, whose fingers always bore traces of the last thing he ate. Garwood took out his handkerchief and polished it away. He was wondering how he would explain the fiasco of the previous evening, and the extravagant squandering of overtime budget to the commander, when his phone rang. He braced himself, sat up straight and straightened his tie. Then he picked up the phone. It wasn't Sir Barnaby — it was Richington-Blythe, and Garwood sensed his fury even before he spoke.

'Jolyon. What can I do for you?'

'Bugger all, apparently, if last night is anything to go by. My bloody wife is allowed to wander, unchallenged, through the vineyard, rotting my grapes, despite half the police force out there looking for her. Then my Master of Wine is attacked, under your very noses. If that's your idea of upholding the law and protecting the community, it isn't mine.'

'I'm very sorry about what happened to Miss Black. It seems it was a failed attempt at a random mugging, rather than a targeted attack. As for your wife, my officers reported that there was no one stalking the vineyards last night. If she had been, she would have been located and arrested.'

'Well, that's just where you're wrong,' Jolyon continued, nastily. 'This morning, my workers reported more damaged grapes, and to add insult to injury, someone had sprayed graffiti on my father's monument. It was her, Gee-Gee, and your woodentops let her get away.'

'Have you any proof it was her?'

'Well, she didn't come in until well after midnight, and when I asked her where she'd been, she laughed at me. How much more proof do you need?'

'What was the graffiti? It might help us to know.'

'Some stupid Bible reference. I've got it written down somewhere.' He shuffled some papers. 'It was "Luke 8:17", whatever that means. How much more of this must I take, before the police get results?'

Garwood was wondering the same thing. 'I already have a man tailing your wife, Jolyon. I'll get his report on where she went last night, and I'll look into the graffiti.'

'Well, see you do, Gee-Gee, or I may have to take this higher. I have a very important event coming up and I can't afford any more trouble.'

* * *

Garwood's interpretation of the chain of command was 'shit rolls downhill.' He stormed into the incident room and shouted, without preamble, 'What the blazes went wrong last night, Dawes? I've had Jolyon Richington-Blythe on the phone, chewing my ear off over our failure to stop his wife damaging more of his grapes. Why didn't we arrest her?'

Jack remained calm. 'Good morning, sir. DC Mitchell is on her tail again today, as we speak. I have his report of her movements last night, if you want to come and have a look?'

Mrs Richington-Blythe left the Hall at 7.30 p.m. She drove to Kings Richington, parked outside Chez Carlene, a bistro on the corner of the high street, and went inside. Her son, Zack, arrived some five minutes later and joined her in the dining area. They ordered several courses and sat eating and chatting.

'DC Mitchell sat at the bar, drinking orange juice and observing, sir, so she was never out of his sight.'

Just before 11 p.m., the son, Zack, got very upset. Mrs Richington-Blythe appeared to be attempting to comfort him, but he stood up, shouted at her and stormed out. Ten minutes later, she paid the bill with a credit card and got up to leave. At no time during the evening did she leave the restaurant, and she did not drink alcohol or I should have prevented her from driving. I followed her back to the Hall. She went inside and did not come out again all night. End of report.

'So she couldn't have been in the vineyard poisoning the grapes or spraying graffiti on the monument. Did Mr Richington-Blythe mention what the graffiti was, sir?'

Having had much of the hot air taken out of his sails, Garwood pulled out the note and read it. 'Luke 8:17.'

Gemma tapped away on her keyboard. 'The King James Bible version says: *For nothing is secret, that shall not be made manifest; neither anything hid, that shall not be known and come abroad.*'

'What's that in plain English, DC Fox?' asked Garwood.

'The modern translation says, *We're not keeping secrets, we're telling them. We're not hiding things, we're bringing everything out into the open.* I'd say someone is threatening to expose Mr Richington-Blythe and his company, sir.'

* * *

117

Corrie was working in the kitchen of one of the Coriander's Cuisine units, on the Kings Richington industrial estate. As business had expanded, so had the need for bigger premises to support it. She now owned several large units and employed a number of staff.

Corrie was extremely proud of Carlene's part in their success. She had started on the very bottom rung of life's ladder but was now a competent and respected chef. Antoine's parents owned a chain of elegant French restaurants called Le Canard Bleu, from which much of the inspiration for Chez Carlene had come. They made the perfect, if unlikely, couple. When the door opened and Carlene hurried in, Corrie could tell from her face that she was bursting to share some juicy gossip.

'Guess who came into the bistro last night, Mrs D.'

'Erm . . . Pac-Man, and he gobbled up all the coasters.'

Carlene giggled. 'No, it was Sandra Richington-Blythe, and she was with her son. Do you remember her from the charity event at the winery? She was the one wearing the little black dress — rather too little, if you ask me. Anyway, Rosie from the Blythe Spirit told me that Zack, that's Rosie's boyfriend, has moved out of Richington Hall, and he has one of the pub guest rooms. This suits her very well because prior to that, they had to do it in the back of his car and it's giving her sciatica, which isn't good if you're a barmaid.' She paused for breath. 'But his mother is still living at the Hall.'

'Is there a point to this? Only, I've got to be at the vicarage with five barley loaves and two smoked mackerel in . . .' She looked at her wrist. 'Blimey, is that the time? This watch has never been the same since it went in the Crème du Barry.'

'Why does the vicar want five loaves and two fish?'

'I didn't ask. I expect he's planning to re-enact something, although you never know. He's a bit avant-garde, so maybe he's going to make a Biblical version of tapas for his CLAP meeting tonight.'

'CLAP?' repeated Carlene. 'Is that like an AA meeting, where people who've been cured share their experience with people who are still trying to get rid of it?'

Corrie giggled. 'Hardly. CLAP stands for Country Ladies' Activities and Pursuits. It's one of the vicar's good works. He likes to present them with new challenges. Next week, they're going to bungee jump off the viaduct. Tell me about Sandra and Zack.'

'Well, you know me, Mrs D. I never eavesdrop on the customers.'

'Course you don't, Carlene. What were they saying?'

'Well, bear in mind I was lip-reading through the glass window of the kitchen door, so it might be a bit mixed-up, what with Antoine's sous-chef chucking all the pots and pans about. Sandra said something like, "Sorry, Zackie, I should have told you before." Then it was mumble, mumble, mumble, and he said, "No, I don't believe it," and looked like he was going to burst into tears. Now, this is the interesting part. She said, "It's true, sweetheart, Jolyon is your father." This next bit was loud and clear. I reckon everyone in Kings Richington heard it, never mind the bistro. He stood up and shouted, "I hate you!" and flounced out. What do you make of that?'

More to the point, Corrie wondered what Jack would make of it, being embroiled as he was in all things Richington-Blythe. 'Well, it kind of explains why Jolyon married a woman half his age. She's the mother of his son.'

* * *

'Yes, we knew,' said Jack, that evening at supper. Corrie was ladling a new version of stew into bowls. As with any new recipes, she was trying it out on Jack first, before adding it to the Cuisine menu. Jack peered at it suspiciously. 'Sandra let it slip when we were questioning her about the attack on Peter Leggett.' He dipped his spoon in and tasted. 'What's this I'm eating?'

'It's Bosnian pot stew, sweetheart. I'm trying out some Balkan recipes.'

'Oh, right.' Jack took another spoonful. 'Sandra didn't want Zack to know about his father, until she was ready to tell him herself. Although, what she's been telling him for the last twenty-three years is anybody's guess.' He paused. 'What are these lumps of green stuff?'

'Bulgarian dumplings. The green bits are spinach. It's a superfood. Look what it did for Popeye. Anyway, according to Carlene, it didn't go down very well. He told her he hated her, in no uncertain terms, and stormed out of the bistro.'

'Yes, Mitch reported it. He doesn't know where Zack went after he left, as his brief was to stick to Sandra.' Jack fished out a chunk of meat. 'Is this beef, pork, lamb or chicken?'

'Yes,' replied Corrie. 'You don't think he came back to Richington Vale village and attacked the Wine Woman?'

'We can't rule it out, although I'd be hard pressed to think of a motive.'

'He was very upset. You would be, if you found out that the man you've hated all your life turns out to be your dad. Maybe, in his confusion, he mistook her for someone else.'

'Maybe. The description would fit, except Suzy said her attacker was all in black with his face covered. And I'm not sure he'd have had the time, even if he broke the speed limit all the way.'

'Easy enough in that big SUV of his. Would you like some Turkish delight for dessert?'

'Only if it has chocolate round it.'

CHAPTER SEVENTEEN

'What I don't understand,' said Gemma, 'is why Sandra Richington-Blythe would want to ruin the vineyard, when she's planning to sue Jolyon for a large part of it. It doesn't make any sense. Surely she'd want him to be worth as much as possible.'

'That's right,' agreed Bugsy. 'Fifty per cent of bugger all is still bugger all. What d'you reckon, guv? Is Jolyon barking up the wrong tree, suspecting Sandra?'

'I believe his judgement is seriously affected by his pathological dislike of her. Think about it. First, she contacts him out of the blue and tells him she's given birth to his son, after what he considered was a mere romp with a tart. She waves the DNA proof at him and demands money. He pays up. Then, eight years later, she turns up on Jolyon's elegant doorstep with said son and threatens to tell everyone, including his family, what he'd been up to, unless he marries her.'

'Hardly likely to endear her to him, was it?' said Bugsy.

'Added to which, I get the impression that Sandra wasn't the only "cocktail waitress" whose services Jolyon paid for during his trips away. He wouldn't want his upmarket friends to hear about it, would he? By their standards, it's OK to indulge in covert, extramarital nookie when you're away from home, but shoving the consequences under people's noses is totally unacceptable.'

'Finally,' continued Bugsy, 'he finds out she's been having naughties with his daughter's partner. Our Sandra has been a thorn in his side for years. He's making accusations to the police in the hopes of getting her arrested, charged and out of his life.'

'Bastard!' exclaimed Gemma. 'I hope she takes him for every penny he's got. Men like him think they can exploit women, by some sort of ancient, feudal law — a kind of *droit du seigneur.*'

'I believe *your* presumptions are showing now, DC Fox,' said Jack. 'Sandra isn't totally without blame. I think she has always had her eye on the main chance, and she has used her son as a bargaining tool.'

'Well, I like her,' said Gemma. 'What you see is what you get. She's fed up with pretending to be something she isn't, and she had the decency to stay away while Jolyon's wife was still alive. I hope it all works out for her.'

A fond hope, but one that unkind fate turned into the kiss of death.

* * *

Jack was still fretting over the fact that someone on his patch had attacked Suzy Black and got away, despite the proximity of a squad of police officers. Richington Vale was hardly an inner city with a terrifying crime rate. It was a rural English village with inquisitive, gossipy inhabitants. Someone must have seen something.

'Bugsy, did anyone leave the Blythe Spirit just before the screaming started?'

Bugsy couldn't answer immediately, due to a mouthful of apple Danish. He hadn't eaten since Iris had cooked him a full English breakfast, and his pastry dependency was kicking in. He swallowed hard and felt it go down in a lump. 'I think the Bartons were the last to go. I remember them shouting goodnight from the door. It was a while after that before we heard the screams, though.'

'Did anyone ask them if they saw a man acting suspiciously? They may have spotted something.' He pictured the layout of the village in his mind. 'The Flower Pot is on the other side of the high street to Miss Black's cottage, only a bit further down.'

'I don't think they were interviewed, guv. D'you want me to send the lad?'

'Yes, please. Ask Aled to take a statement. You never know. It could throw up something useful.'

* * *

When Aled pushed open the door of the Flower Pot, he was enveloped by the cool, floral ambience. He reckoned it must be nice to work in that atmosphere. Some of the smells you were exposed to as a police officer were decidedly above and beyond his pay grade, and that included being upwind of Sergeant Malone when he'd had baked beans for lunch. Unfortunately, the pollen triggered his hay fever, and he began sneezing, violently.

Sheila Barton was making up small bunches of cottage garden pinks for the church. It was her turn to decorate the pews, and pinks gave the church such a lovely scent. She looked up as Aled sneezed. 'Oh dear, hay fever? Well, at least nobody ever died from it,' she said comfortingly.

Aled sneezed again, several times. 'They reckon my great-great-grandmother did.' He pulled out a handful of tissues. 'She was taking tea in a botanical conservatory in Pontypridd and sneezed herself through a plate-glass window. Sliced her bustle clean off.'

'Oh dear,' said Sheila. There really was no helpful reply to that. 'What can I get you today? A bouquet or a plant? Is it for your mum or your girlfriend? If it's your girlfriend, I suggest a romantic bunch of red roses. If it's your mum, they usually prefer a plant.'

'Detective Constable Williams, Miss Barton.' Aled produced his warrant card. 'I wonder if I might ask you some questions.'

'Certainly officer. I'm guessing you're part of DI Dawes's team. How can I help?'

'It's about the night Miss Black was attacked. I understand you and your brother were in the Blythe Spirit, before the assault occurred.'

'That's right. What a terrible thing to happen. One of many, just lately. Poor DI Dawes must be struggling to keep pace with it.'

You don't know the half of it, thought Aled. 'As this shop is almost opposite Miss Black's cottage, give or take a few yards, and you had left the pub to walk home, we wondered if you had seen anything suspicious? Anyone loitering in the shadows or in a shop doorway?'

She didn't answer immediately. Trying to cast her mind back, Aled assumed.

'No, I'm sorry, constable. All was quiet when we reached the shop. We let ourselves in, went up to our flat and made some cocoa. Then we went to our rooms. We each like to spend a few minutes in private prayer before we retire. That was when we heard the screaming. By the time we came out to see what was going on, DI Dawes and Sergeant Malone were already there.'

'What did you do then?'

'I wondered if we should offer some help, but seconds later, a plain-clothes lady officer and a number of uniformed constables arrived. Miles said we'd just get in the way. We did think about taking some flowers round, but Sébastien Richington-Blythe came into the shop the next day and bought a huge bouquet for her. I don't think there's anything else I can tell you.'

'Might your brother have seen something?'

She shook her head. 'I doubt it, or he would have mentioned it.'

'Perhaps I could have a word with Mr Barton?'

'He isn't here right now, officer. I believe he's on his way to our market garden. You might catch him there.'

* * *

After Aled had gone, Miles came out from behind the door, where he'd been listening. 'Do you think the police are on to us?'

'No, of course not. How could they be? They wouldn't have sent a detective constable if they suspected anything. It was just a perfectly routine enquiry.'

'Perhaps we should finish what we came here to do and go — quickly.'

'Absolutely not. We've been planning this for a long time, and we're going to do it properly. Stop panicking, Miles. I have everything under control.'

* * *

Sandra had been aware of DC Mitchell five minutes after he started following her. After all, it wasn't the first time she'd had the Old Bill on her tail. In her shoplifting days, she'd been able to outrun them, but she didn't fancy her chances now, not in these shoes.

At first, she had found it amusing and she would wave to him, to let him know he had been spotted. But after a while, it became tedious. She was planning a shopping trip to buy some new clothes and she certainly didn't want him hanging around like a bad smell, waiting for her to come out of the loo or the changing rooms. She had an idea to shake him off. If she hid where he couldn't find her, eventually he'd get fed up. He'd tell Dawes that he'd lost her and push off. Then she'd come out and get on with her day. She knew the ideal place to give him the slip. He'd never find her there. She'd take her bottle of vodka and have a couple of nips, maybe even a snooze, while she waited for him to go.

* * *

Jack's phone rang. It was DC Mitchell. 'I'm sorry, sir. I've lost Mrs Richington-Blythe. One minute she was here, then suddenly she'd vanished.' Mitch was despondent. Rarely had he lost a 'mark' he'd been assigned to follow. It was failure in his eyes. 'I followed her, at a distance, into the vineyard. I thought she'd just gone for a stroll in the sunshine, to watch the grape harvest. Next thing, she'd disappeared. I walked up and down the rows of vines, thinking she'd pop out suddenly and go "Boo". It was the kind of thing she would do. But there's no sign of her. Now Sébastien has arrived with a group of tourists, and he's showing them the harvesting process.'

'OK, Mitch. Come back in. We'll pick her up again tomorrow, although I'm not sure if we're following her because Jolyon Richington-Blythe still believes she's killing his vines or for her own protection.'

* * *

Sébastien spread his arms in an expansive gesture. 'This, ladies and gentlemen, is how our grapes are harvested. Here, you can watch state-of-the-art technology at work. But please don't get too close, as this is powerful machinery.'

Sébastien was taking only a handful of tourists around the vineyard. The numbers had dwindled drastically since news of the deaths of people associated with the vineyard had appeared in the *Echo*. Indeed, the editor had written his own piece about how he'd actually been present when a respected senior of the village, the retired primary school teacher, had been poisoned in the Richington-Blythe events suite. Then, when the news of McKendrick's stabbing was leaked — the second vineyard manager to die in a matter of weeks — potential visitors had split into two camps. Those who wouldn't go near the place, and those whose morbid curiosity had been aroused. Sébastien thought he recognized the chippy lad who had witnessed Beacham with his head jammed in the storage tank. Having been issued with a replacement ticket, he was obviously determined to get his money's worth.

'These mighty harvesters have on-board destemming technology. As you can see, each harvester has two bins. Each bin can hold at least two tons of fruit before it needs to be emptied. Once they're full, the harvested grapes are then emptied into an asymmetrical hopper, called a gondola. The one you're looking at contains some five tons of grapes.' There were murmurs of astonishment.

'The technological advantage of the gondola in bringing grapes from the vineyard to the winery,' Sébastien continued, 'is its ability to hydraulically lift itself to dump the grapes into a truck-trailer. This hauls the grapes away to be processed at the winery. Watch carefully, ladies and gentlemen, the dumping of five tons of grapes is quite spectacular.'

Sébastien motioned to the worker and the gondola began to slowly lift and tip. Grapes poured into the truck until the gondola was nearly empty. It was then that the dead body of a woman was flung from its depths, like a limp rag doll, onto the mountain of grapes below.

There were gasps of horror. Even the chippy lad, who had witnessed Bob's death in the storage chamber, was subdued. 'Blimey!' he whispered. 'That's what I call a sticky end.'

CHAPTER EIGHTEEN

'You do realize that this is number five, Inspector,' observed
Dr Hardacre.

Jack and Bugsy were gowned up and observing at Sandra
Richington-Blythe's post-mortem. 'Are we aiming for a
round half-dozen? Only, the coroner is getting fidgety. He
likes to spend a fortnight in Bognor, once the summer's over,
and the cases are building up. As this rate, it'll be Christmas
before he gets to roll up the coronial trouser-leg and dip a toe
in the sub-zero waves.'

'I'd like to say that this lady is the last one, Doctor, but
who knows?' Jack was morose.

'It's the first one I've had covered in squashed grapes,'
she replied.

'Is that what killed her, Doc?' asked Bugsy.

'Pardon me if I sound facetious, Sergeant, but you try
climbing out from under five tons of grapes. Especially with
half a bottle of vodka inside you. She only drank the good
stuff, mind — wheat grain and spring water. All the same,
her liver was in a bad way.'

'So it was a toss-up what would kill her first, the grape
or the grain,' quipped Bugsy. 'And the grape won.'

'And your gallows humour will be the death of you, Sergeant,' she fired back.

'Any sign of violence before the grape avalanche?' asked Jack.

'Difficult to be sure, but I'd say not. No sign of blunt force trauma or manhandling. No broken nails or specific bruising. In my opinion, cause of death was straight suffocation. At a guess, I'd say she climbed in there herself — for whatever reason — because she'd taken off her shoes. Then, she either fell asleep or passed out. The grapes did the rest. Obviously, your inquiries will establish why she would want to hide in a hopper.'

WIFE OF MILLIONAIRE WINEMAKER CRUSHED BY GRAPES, screamed the headline of the *Richington Echo. The body of Sandra Richington-Blythe, 41, was discovered, barefoot, beneath five tons of grapes, during a guided tour of the vineyard. Onlookers believe it may have been a grape-treading demonstration gone badly wrong.*

Jack reckoned he already knew why she'd climbed into the hopper — to shake off Mitch. Jack was angry. Sandra had died because of Jolyon Richington-Blythe's paranoia about her poisoning his precious vines, compounded with Garwood's anxiety to placate the Worshipful Master of his lodge so that he might be the next person elected to high office.

Gemma was angry, too. 'It isn't right, sir. The woman might not have been the Richington-Blythes' idea of a lady, and some might judge her morals, but she hadn't broken the law. She didn't deserve to die.'

'I agree, Gemma, but unfortunately there is no one we can hold directly responsible for her death. The health and safety people will have a field day, but the coroner will more than likely determine accidental death or return a narrative verdict.'

'Is it down to us to notify her son?' asked Aled.

'I expect the grapevine will already have done that,' said Bugsy. 'No pun intended.'

'The poor lad will be devastated.' Gemma felt truly sorry for him.

* * *

When Zack found out what had happened to his mother, he wasn't just devastated, he was out of his mind with grief and anger. His mother had been the only person he'd ever loved. The only person who'd ever loved him, until he'd met Rosie. She'd been there for him his whole life, and much as he hated living at Richington Hall, he knew she'd taken him there so that he could have a good education at a private school and a decent future. Things she couldn't give him on her own.

He was convinced that Jolyon, his father — although he would never acknowledge him as such — had deliberately thrown Sandra in the hopper, knowing she would be killed. Zack knew about the pending divorce petition and how such a payout would finish the failing vineyard. Jolyon cared more about his father's precious legacy than anyone or anything.

He tracked Jolyon down in the tasting room, admiring his trophies. He was actually polishing the gold label on one of the display magnums, just hours after Sandra had been found. Zack crashed through the door and flew at him, grasping the lapels on his fancy jacket. 'You murdered my mother, you bastard, and now I'm going to make you pay.'

'Your mother was a tart, a faithless bitch and a gold digger. And if anyone was born a bastard, it's you.' Jolyon tried to push him off. It was a mistake.

Zack propelled Jolyon backwards into a display cabinet, breaking the glass with his head and drawing first blood. Jolyon was stocky but, at his age, no match for a fit twenty-three-year-old, mad for revenge. The beating was primitive and one-sided. Everything that makes humans rational lives in the prefrontal cortex of the brain. Zack's was switched off.

'No one stands by and watches someone get killed, unless they're a cowardly murderer, like you.' Zack threw his right fist in a curved punch at Jolyon's jaw then followed it up with a sickening blow to the stomach. Jolyon tried to speak, to call for help, but he was winded and gasping for his next breath. Zack pulled him to his feet by the despised fancy lapels and propped him against the wall. He reached back his fist to deliver the killer punch, intending to smash Jolyon's face straight into the back of his skull. But just as he took aim, a hand closed around his wrist, pulling him off balance.

'That's enough, son. He's had enough.' Bugsy steered Zack away. For a moment, Zack looked like he was going to swing a punch. 'I wouldn't, if I were you. I might look portly, but I promise you, I can punch my weight.' Zack finally seemed to regain his wits. Realizing the imprudence of punching a police officer, he sank down on one of the viewing benches.

It was Marianne who had raised the alarm. Zack had pushed past her, madness in his eyes, and made for the tasting room, where he knew Jolyon would be at this time of day. Unable to stop him, she had telephoned MIT for help. Now, she was on her knees beside her father, mopping the blood, fearing for his weak heart. 'Papa, are you OK? Zack didn't know what he was doing. He's grieving for his mother. Why does he hate you so?'

'Because he's my son.' Jolyon whispered, then he passed out cold.

'What?' Sébastien had hurried in behind Marianne. 'He can't be. Is that true, Zack?' Are you really our half-brother?'

Zack had his head in his hands. 'Yes, but I wish to God I wasn't.'

Jack, hovering in the background of the action, had telephoned for an ambulance. He guessed he should arrest Zack but he didn't. Nobody had died and this family was already in turmoil. He wasn't going to make it any worse, unless Jolyon insisted on pressing charges when he recovered.

* * *

'It was a real fistfight, then?' Corrie had heard rumours, but waited until Jack got home for the witness account.

'It was real, all right. I think Zack would have killed Jolyon if we hadn't stopped him.' He stole one of the chips Corrie had just emptied into a bowl. 'Blimey! Chips! It'll be fish fingers next. Are we on an economy drive?'

'They're not chips, they're triple-cooked fries with parmesan and truffle oil.' She stopped him as he reached for the condiments. 'Don't you dare drench them in salt and vinegar.'

'What about ketchup?'

'I shan't even dignify that with a reply. I feel sorry for Zack. It's a good job he has Rosie. Carlene says she's genuinely fond of him. Apparently, he's helping to run the pub. Matt says he was doing really well until this happened.'

'I don't expect he'll ever go back to live at the Hall,' said Jack.

'Maybe Matt will give him a permanent job. They always seem rushed off their feet when Matt's down in the cellar fiddling with the barrels, leaving Rosie to cope on her own.'

'The pub is part of the Richington-Blythe estate. It depends what the family decides to do with it.' Jack didn't have great expectations of the Richington-Blythes' business acumen, even less of their altruism.

'Speaking as someone in the hospitality sector, I reckon it's a nice little earner. They say the craft ale is one of the best, so with the award-winning sparkling Chardonnay and Freddy's cooking, they do very well. If Jolyon shuts them down out of vindictiveness, he'll be cutting off a lively, lucrative nose to spite his financially exhausted face.'

'That's a very peculiar analogy, sweetheart, but I know what you mean.' Jack was ravenous and hoping there'd be something recognizable to go with the fancy chips. 'He's a good bloke, Matt. Always ready to help out and support local causes.'

'I agree. Every village should have a Matt.' She grinned. 'You can uncross your fingers. It's steak.'

* * *

They kept Jolyon in the private hospital for a few days. As the doctor pointed out, he was no longer young, he had a congenital heart problem and he'd taken quite a beating. In the end, he discharged himself, anxious to finalize arrangements for the visiting French multinational wine producer. Like the Richington-Blythe winery, this company had started out as family-owned, but now, some seventy years later, it manufactured, exported and sold wine, beers, spirits and mineral water internationally, through its subsidiaries. Jolyon was confident their investment would change the fortunes of his winery.

He called a board meeting, which was sparse, with just himself, Sébastien and Marianne. He invited Suzy Black to join them. Her professional qualification would go a long way to impressing the visitors, there being only around four hundred Masters of Wine globally.

They looked a meagre group with just four of them spread out around the big conference table in the boardroom. Marianne was far from happy that her father had left the care of the hospital. 'Papa, you're still weak. You should be lying down.'

Sébastien was more pragmatic. 'Father, your injuries will still be visible when the French consortium arrives. We can't tell them you were beaten up by your son.'

'I'm still looking fairly battered and bruised, too,' admitted Suzy.

Jolyon had it covered. 'I shall tell them we were in a car accident. It's perfectly plausible.' He turned to Marianne. 'Have all the arrangements been made for the catering and decoration of the tasting rooms?'

'*Oui*, Papa. I have engaged Coriander's Cuisine as usual. They are bringing a French-speaking chef, as well as their usual staff. If any of the visitors don't speak English, he will be on hand to translate information about the food — vegan, allergies and such. The Flower Pot is to provide floral arrangements as well as the Dionysus display that was so much admired at the charity event.'

'The storage tanks are all full to capacity. It might be impressive to take them down to the cellars to see the extent of our production and last year's fermenting vintage,' suggested Sébastien.

'Good thinking. What I want to avoid, at all costs, is any hint of the unfortunate accidents that have occurred recently. We don't want the French to think they are investing in an ill-fated vineyard. Nothing must come out about the deaths, never mind the rumours that some may have been murders. Is that clear to everyone?'

They nodded, all except for Suzy. 'Jolyon, I appreciate you don't want your guests to hear tittle-tattle, and we could probably explain away the deaths of Bob Beacham, Doctor Anstruther and even Miss Chambers, but won't it be awkward explaining why the vineyard manager was found with a pruning knife sticking out of his chest? And your wife's part in that? And now she's had a fatal accident, too. That's an awful lot of coincidences for one winery, don't you think? To an outsider, it might almost look like someone is deliberately trying to ruin you.'

Jolyon sighed. 'Suzy, somehow I have to pull off this deal. Otherwise, the wine heritage that I have fought my whole life to maintain will all have been for nothing.'

He looked so desperate and downcast, she almost felt sorry for him. Almost.

CHAPTER NINETEEN

Clive was already in and waiting for Jack the following morning. He looked tired, as if he'd been working most of the night.

'Sir, do you remember asking me to trawl through the information I copied from Doctor Anstruther's medical records? We discussed the balance of probabilities. You wanted me to look for cases where compensation might have been payable, if the doctor hadn't misdiagnosed the illness or cause of death.'

'I remember. Did you have any luck?'

'Not at first. Doctor Anstruther kept two sets of records for winery employees. The first set covered incidents like babies being born, children's ailments, cuts from pruning knives, ordinary everyday accidents and illnesses that occur in every workforce. The second set was encrypted.'

'But you got in, anyway,' predicted Jack.

'That's what I'm paid for, sir. It took me most of the night.'

'I'm guessing that's where you found the unorthodox stuff.'

'Correct. Over the years, there have been disproportionately high numbers of employees suffering and sometimes dying from respiratory diseases. There were also musculoskeletal problems, especially of the wrists and hands, from vine-pruning work, and allergic diseases, including occupational asthma, from exposure to pesticides on the growing vines. At this point, I felt much of what I'd found was outside my sphere of expertise, so early this morning, I consulted Doctor Hardacre for her opinion.'

'Blimey,' said Bugsy. He'd come in via the canteen and was munching a bacon roll and carrying a coffee to go. 'The meeting of two massive geek minds. I'm surprised we mere mortals didn't feel the shock waves.'

Clive grinned. 'It didn't take her long to find evidence of back and neck strains as well as — and I quote — "a variety of tendinopathies and neuropathies of the upper extremities". She said that pruning vines, making more than thirty cuts per minute, "can produce significant biomechanical strains because of the repetitive actions, forceful motions and awkward postures required." But here's the most relevant bit.' He peered more closely at his screen. 'I'm reading the doctor's words here: "A variety of pesticides are used to control pests, including organophosphates, pyrethroids, fungicides and herbicides. Each pesticide group has its own specific toxicity profile. The most important routes of occupational exposure are inhalation and dermal absorption."' He looked up. 'In Doctor Hardacre's view, viticulture workers should be monitored regularly for exposure, and if they exhibit toxic effects, they should be removed from any further pesticide exposure and their work practices should be reassessed.'

'Like Jolyon is going to do that,' Gemma scorned. 'Think what it would do to his productivity, never mind the reputation of his precious winery.' She frowned. 'Isn't there a viticulture workers' union?'

'Not specifically,' said Clive, 'but there's a self-appointed bloke who purports to uphold workers' rights.'

'Well, what's he doing about all this flagrant flouting of employment law?'

'Keeping his mouth shut and taking regular backhanders from management,' replied Clive. 'I hacked into his bank account. If anyone asks him about joining a bona fide union, he probably tells them they're best off with him, as anything else will cost them money.'

Gemma was red in the face with outrage. 'I don't believe it. What century are we in?'

Jack could see her point, and no doubt the proper authorities would have something to say about it, but primarily, he wanted information that would assist with his murder investigations. 'Did you find any potential suspects among the encrypted files? Victims who might want to bring down Richington-Blythe and his entire empire?'

'Plenty, sir, but many of them are dead, and there weren't any details of what happened to their dependants. One name was a surprise, though. Dominique Richington-Blythe, Jolyon's first wife and Sébastien and Marianne's mother. She died at the age of forty-nine. According to the death certificate, signed by Anstruther, she died of pneumonia and complications.'

'Wasn't there an inquest?' asked Aled.

'No need. She was under the doctor for at least the last fortnight of her life and died, he said, from natural causes. Doctor Hardacre reckons that given the circumstances and symptoms leading up to her death, it was almost certainly pesticide poisoning, like the others.'

'His own wife!' Gemma was incensed. 'The man's a monster.'

Jack nodded. 'That might well be the case, but my copper's nose is telling me that our five deaths are leading up to the big one — Jolyon's. However much we think he deserves it, it's our job to ensure it doesn't happen. Keep digging, Clive. See if you can track down anybody still alive and with a grudge.'

* * *

Miles Barton was in his happy place — his flower garden. Asters, carnations, gerberas and phlox flourished alongside one another in a riot of glorious autumn colours. Sheila had walked down to the market garden with a flask of tea and scones, leaving the shop with a sign saying "Back soon". It was a common practice in Richington Vale's village shops when someone needed to pop out briefly.

They sat in companionable silence, drinking tea in the dying sunshine for a while, then Miles asked, 'When will we finish it, Sheila?'

'Soon,' she said. 'Just one last push. We've already done the most important part.'

'And then the nightmares will stop?'

'Yes. Then, we'll just get on with our lives. Remember, Miles, this isn't just for us. It's for all the others as well.'

'I know. I just want to get it over with.' Miles wasn't as confident as Sheila. He never had been. He had always drawn his strength from her, even as children.

'We have that big event coming up soon at the winery. We'll do the floral decorations and set up the Dionysus display with the grapes and vines. We'll finish it after that.'

'Good. Shall we stay here in Richington Vale, once it's over?'

'It would be nice. I've got the shop, you've got this market garden that you love. It depends whether they connect us to what we've already done. I don't see why they should. We've been very careful. Of course, the vicar will be devastated when he finds out, but that can't be helped, I'm afraid. We just need to hold our nerve, finish what we started and then we'll decide.'

* * *

Desperate for any morsel of intelligence about Richington Vale that might assist with his inquiries, Jack wondered what the fight in the pub car park had been about.

'Bugsy, when we first discussed the village, I asked you if there had ever been any trouble.'

'That's right, guv. I remembered Uniform had been called out to break up a fight outside in the pub car park. Just the usual drunken brawl that got out of hand.'

'Can you remember who was involved?'

'Not really. Norman and his lads handled it. Shall I ask him?'

'Yes, please. I'm clutching at straws — but you never know. If I'm lucky, this straw might just turn out to be a long one, instead of the short one I usually draw.'

Sergeant Parsloe came up to the MIT room to read out his record of the incident. 'I'm not sure if any of this is relevant, Jack, but a significant engagement took place between the vicar and Robbie McKendrick. It ended up with a fight involving the pub landlord, most of Richington Vale bowls club, a retired dance teacher and two elderly ladies from the vicar's MAP class.'

'What's a MAP class?' asked Gemma.

'Martial Arts for Pensioners,' replied Norman. 'They man the doors at church jumble sales. Anyway, when things got out of hand, the police were called — that would have been me and Constable Johnson — and we broke it up.'

'Can you remember how it started, Norman?'

'Not personally, but I took statements from the witnesses. It seems McKendrick was in the pub with Marianne Richington-Blythe. He was drunk and started an argument with her. Of course, her being a lady, she wouldn't rise to it, which made him even nastier. The reverend was having a quiet pint with some friends, but when McKendrick started threatening Marianne physically, he felt he should step in on her behalf. McKendrick told him to "sod off", or words to that effect, and was daft enough to swing a punch. The reverend dodged it, but McKendrick kept on trying and missing. They danced around each other for a bit, ducking and diving, with technical coaching from the retired ballet teacher, who allegedly shouted, "Never mind the *pas de deux*, vicar, punch his bloody lights out."'

There was stifled laughter around the room.

'Eventually, fed up with warning him, the reverend put McKendrick down with a single right hook that lifted him a good two feet off the ground and broke his jaw. It later turned out that he'd been middleweight champion of his university and considered a bit tasty in the ring. By then, the rest of the drunken village idiots had started a free-for-all outside, most of 'em not having a clue what they were fighting about. We put a couple of them in a cell to cool down. During the affray, Constable Johnson sustained a blow to his right ear, thought to be from a handbag, but no charges were ever brought. That was it, really — or it would have been, if McKendrick hadn't reported it to the bishop.'

'That's interesting, Norman,' said Jack, who hadn't realized village life was so high-spirited. 'So McKendrick might have had a grudge against the vicar for making him look a berk, and vice versa, for getting him into trouble with the bishop?'

'I suppose so, but if you're thinking the vicar might have knifed him, you're completely wrong. The reverend wouldn't harm anyone. He doesn't have a temper on him — if you ignore the killer right hook and his flaming-red hair.'

CHAPTER TWENTY

There was just a week to go before the French conglomerate — Le Monde du Vin — was due to arrive. Jolyon was on edge, desperate for the investment that was to save his winery. No expense would be spared to convince them that they would see excellent returns on their money. Jolyon's chief accountant, also a lodge member, had prepared the accounts creatively — not actually lying, but presenting the finances in the best possible light. Now it was down to the staff and workers to showcase the vineyards at their best.

Jolyon hadn't appointed a new manager. Strangely, there hadn't been much enthusiasm for the job. It was decided that Sébastien would continue in the role until the future had been secured. Neither had he been able to secure a doctor to oversee the vine workers' health in the way that he wished. The Griffin fellow had behaved very strangely when he'd been told the conditions of the job. Jolyon couldn't understand it. The man stood to make good money, but he'd turned it down flat. He decided to wait until the visit was over, then he'd look for someone more amenable.

An army of cleaners had been brought in to ensure every surface, every dark corner of the Hall and winery, gleamed with apparent prosperity. Outside, the dead vines had been cleared away and ploughing — turning the soil between the rows and partially covering the vines to protect them from winter frosts — had started early, to give the impression of progressive thinking. It also avoided the need to explain what had happened to the dead ones. But the most important part of the visit, the aspect that would most influence the French winemakers, was the Richington Vale sparkling Chardonnay.

'Suzy, do you have everything ready for the grand tasting of last year's vintage?' Jolyon had no doubt that she would, despite her recent ordeal, as she was a consummate professional. She was also very attractive, which, in Jolyon's view, could only be an advantage in a presentation situation. Clever use of make-up had concealed her facial injuries, which hadn't been serious.

'Stop worrying, Jolyon, it's going to be very special, I promise. You must feel sad that Dominique won't be here to share this moment in your remarkable wine life. Sébastien tells me his mother put so much work into the vineyard in the early days — as, I imagine, did many others.'

Jolyon ignored that and went off on another tack entirely. 'I wish the old air commodore, my father, were here to see me restore his vineyard to its former glory. I must continue his dream, Suzy. It's the only thing that matters to me. You will help me, won't you, dear? I'll make it worth your while.' He put a casual hand on her bottom.

'Oh yes, Jolyon. I'll be right there beside you when it all kicks off.'

* * *

Suzy was rehearsing her digital presentation when Sébastien came in and closed the door behind him. He had an earnest look on his face. 'Suzy, I want to proposition you.'

She smiled, mockingly. 'I think your father just beat you to it.'

'What?' He looked confused.

'Never mind. What's the proposition?'

'Father doesn't know this yet, but when the French have invested and the winery is secure again, I'm leaving for California. I've accepted a job in a massive Napa Valley vineyard. It's way beyond anything I could achieve here. The thing is, I want you to come with me — as my wife.'

She showed no sign of emotion. 'I realize this is a cliché, but isn't it rather sudden?'

'You must know how I feel about you, how I've felt since you first joined us. I know it was only a short while ago, but I think I've always loved you. Father agrees that it's an excellent idea. I guess he's hoping for a grandson, to carry on the Richington-Blythe name and brand.'

'Really? Well, that's all right, then. As long as Jolyon approves.'

The sarcasm was lost on him. 'Does that mean you'll marry me?' Excited, he went to take something from his pocket.

Suzy feared it might be a ring. *Dear God, please don't let him get down on one knee.* She pre-empted it. 'Whoa! At least let me think about it. Give me until this event is over. Then, if you still want to marry me, I'll give you an answer.'

He left, looking a little deflated, but by no means defeated.

* * *

Le Monde du Vin arrived in full force, bringing with them their own experts at buying, selling and marketing wine, plus a viticulture director and a brand ambassador. Astute and forward-looking, they had no intention of ploughing money into a vineyard that would not enhance the profile of their own brand. Jolyon was a man in torment — needing the money that the French could invest, but at the same time resenting any hint of a takeover. These were the types of winemakers that his father had wanted to challenge and eclipse, not join in partnership, but it was that or admit total failure.

Richington Hall was full, with every bedroom and suite occupied. Extra staff had been recruited from the village to work in the kitchens, dining room and bedrooms. It was expensive, but Jolyon did not want the visitors to pick up any hint of desperation or penny-pinching. There was, of course, one final, last-ditch option open to him, but while it would benefit the village, it would mean the end of Richington Vale Winery, so it was out of the question and not to be contemplated. Even Sébastien and Marianne were unaware of it, and for Jolyon, it was vital that it should remain that way.

By the end of the week, the prospective investors had been all over every inch of the vineyard's business. They were inscrutable and asked many questions, but provided no clues as to their intentions. On the last night, there was to be a grand presentation, designed to put the final gloss on the whole enterprise.

Dinner was over and the French had been extravagantly wined and dined with a seven-course menu devised by Corrie and her team, to compliment the Gold Label sparkling Chardonnay. Now it was time for Jolyon's last pitch — an exposition, extolling Richington Vale Winery as marketable and consumer-driven, and listing the unquestionable advantages of ploughing a considerable amount of money into the company.

Corrie and Carlene, having completed a triumph of catering, were relaxing in the wings, namely a corner of the room, where they weren't conspicuous.

'How is Jolyon holding up, do you think?' whispered Corrie.

'Nervous as a novice in a knocking shop,' Carlene whispered back, in her usual graphic manner. 'He's been to the loo three times in the last half-hour.'

The presentation was timed for nine o'clock. The technical equipment was set up and there were ripples of anticipation among the audience, seated around tables in the main events suite. Each table bore a striking, floral centrepiece, created by Sheila and Miles, with the emphasis on grapes and greenery. Many local VIPs had been invited, including Chief Superintendent George Garwood and Cynthia, and the editor of the *Richington Echo*, who went unaccompanied as his wife had insisting on staying home to worm the cat.

At the back of the suite, Jack, Bugsy, Aled and Gemma were sitting in a row, trying not to look like a caricature of coppers, but failing.

'No chance of a beer, I suppose,' wondered Bugsy. 'This fizzy stuff makes me fart.'

'What exactly are we doing here, sir?' asked Aled.

'Jolyon requested an unobtrusive police presence,' replied Jack.

'Why? Is he expecting a demonstration by the Temperance Society, waving placards, denouncing the demon drink?' Gemma half hoped something would happen to put a spanner in Jolyon's works. As a police officer, it was her job to protect him. As an ordinary human being, she wanted to give him a lecture on *noblesse oblige*.

'I'm not sure what he's expecting, Gemma,' said Jack, 'but the Dawes "nose" is twitching. I have a feeling of foreboding.'

Nobody spoke after that. When DI Dawes had a foreboding feeling, you could bet your life something unpleasant was about to happen. He was rarely wrong.

* * *

At five minutes to nine, the subdued lighting blazed into full brightness, and an operatic tenor began singing loudly in the background.

In the corner by the speakers, Corrie jumped. 'Blimey, what's that?'

'It's the "Champagne Aria" from *Don Giovanni* by Wolfgang Amadeus Mozart.'

Corrie was impressed. 'Well done, Carlene. How did you know that?'

'It's written here, on the back of this menu card. Personally, I'd have thought "Little Ole Wine Drinker Me" would've been more appropriate. At least we could have joined in the chorus.'

Corrie agreed. 'Never mind. Once Jolyon's done his turn, we can all go home. My feet are killing me.'

All alone in the gents', collecting his thoughts, Jolyon was making the final adjustments to his appearance, straightening his bow tie — hand-tied, he couldn't bear those cheap ones on elastic — and polishing his already-gleaming shoes on the backs of his trousers. He was as ready as he could be for what he believed was the biggest challenge of his life. The music that Suzy had activated was his cue to go out onto the podium and deliver. His heart, often erratic, was pounding. He pushed open the door and strode purposefully towards the events suite.

He never got there. As he passed the tasting room, a hand holding a magnum of Richington Vale Gold Label sparkling Chardonnay snaked out and welted him over the head with it.

Expectations had been raised, along with the lights and the music, but when Jolyon still hadn't appeared by nine thirty, people began shuffling their feet and talking among themselves.

Marianne became anxious. 'Sébastien, where is Papa? He should be on.'

'I thought he was with you. I can't find Suzy, either.' Sébastien was anxious. It was so unlike Suzy to just go off somewhere on an important occasion. She was meticulous about her duties, and had been an enormous asset to the company, which was why he wanted her to marry him and come with him to his new job in California. 'Something must have happened to them. You go back to the house, see if they're there,' he suggested. 'I'll search the winery rooms.'

By ten o'clock, neither Jolyon nor Suzy had appeared. Le Monde du Vin had had a long day, and one by one, they began drifting off to their rooms, ready for an early start back to France next morning. They were clearly unimpressed with the failure of the owner to appear, considering that this was his final opportunity to appeal for investment.

The editor of the *Echo* was already wording his article for the next day: *Jolyon Richington-Blythe fails to consolidate his appeal for French funds. Is this the end of Richington Vale Winery as we know it?*

CHAPTER TWENTY-ONE

When Jolyon regained consciousness, he was aware of two things — a pounding head and aching limbs. Gradually, he became aware of his surroundings. It was cold and dark. The night air and the smell of vegetation told him he was outdoors. Buy why? Wasn't he supposed to be giving a presentation? His memory was drifting back. He must hurry. He needed to save his vineyard.

It was when he tried to stand up that he realized he couldn't move. He was tied to some sort of rustic seat. What the hell was going on?

'Can he hear us, Sam?' asked Michael.

'Yes, Mikey, he can hear us now.'

'I thought I might have hit him too hard.'

'No, it was exactly right,' she said. Then, to Jolyon, 'You were out just long enough for us to drag your miserable carcass into the centre of your father's precious maze, where no one will find your body for a very long time. With any luck, they'll just find your putrefied corpse, tied to this bench — or what's left of it after the crows have finished with you. By then, we'll be long gone.'

Jolyon's head was still spinning. He couldn't see the woman in the dark, but he thought he recognized her voice. 'Who is that? What's happening?'

'My name is Samantha Baker. This is my brother, Michael. You won't remember us, of course. We were just two urchins from the village who weren't considered good enough to play with your children, in their smart private school uniforms and talking in fancy French accents. We village kids used to sneak up here and play in this maze.'

'Clever of you to remember the way round it, after all these years, Sam,' said Michael. 'But then you always were the clever one, working out what we needed to do to change our names and come back here to be accepted into the community.'

'Not just accepted,' corrected Sam, 'but popular. Everybody likes us. We could have settled here permanently. Not now, of course, because we're going to kill you.' Her tone was quite matter-of-fact. 'Did you know your dopey son is going away to work in a Californian winery? Once you're dead, which will be in about two minutes, that'll be the end of the Richington-Blythe wine dynasty for ever.'

Jolyon thought he was going mad. His heart felt like it was in his throat. 'But why? What have I ever done to you?'

She laughed. 'I could say, "How long have you got?" but I already know how long you've got, so I'll explain. I shouldn't want you to die without knowing why. I was ten when Thomas Baker, our father, died. Mikey here was only seven. Dad had worked for you all his adult life. Our mother was destitute. No money and no home, and you didn't care. Your corrupt doctor said smoking had killed Dad, when he knew it was the pesticides.'

'But I finally put a stop to Anstruther,' said Michael, proudly.

Jolyon gasped. 'Oh God. You ran him over.'

'You bet, I did.' Michael laughed. 'You should have heard the crunch before he went flying through the air. I did away with Beacham, too. He knew what had killed our dad but he said it was smoking, because you paid him, and because he wanted the manager's job.'

'I was sorry about poor old Potty Chambers, though, but she remembered me, unfortunately for her,' Sam explained.

'It was the scar on my neck when I fell off the swings at school. She took me to hospital to have it stitched. She was a canny old girl and I knew she'd remember, eventually, so I had to put a stop to her.'

'Robbie caught me poisoning the grapes in your vineyard and recognized me straight away,' said Michael. 'Not surprising. He'd seen me enough times in the village. So he had to go as well. It was just bad luck, really. He'd been inside that hut all night, shagging your wife and drinking your wine, and next morning, there he was, standing there pissing, just as I was passing. You should have seen the look of surprise on his face when I stuck the knife in his chest.'

'Sandra?' whispered Jolyon, weakly.

'No, that was an accident. The grapes killed her, not us,' said Sam. 'Ghastly woman, though. I guess you were glad to be shot of her. You see, Jolyon, what we're doing could be considered a public service. It's retribution for all those workers who should have received help and compensation but were tricked out of it, and ended up dead or suffering in poverty. Although I don't suppose DI Dawes will see it like that, so we won't be hanging around to explain.' She patted the old man's shoulder condescendingly. 'Well, it's been nice chatting, Jolyon, but it's late and we still have work to do, after we've finished with you. Show him the knife, Mikey.'

Michael reached up and flicked on his head torch. 'This belonged to our father.' He held up an old, well-used pruning knife. 'Dad was an expert. He could make more than thirty cuts a minute, deadly accurate. I don't possess his skills, so I'll only be making one cut. It might not be accurate, but it will definitely be deadly.'

Jolyon struggled to free himself, but the ropes were too tight. He was helpless. As Michael approached and put the blade to his throat, he could feel his heart racing. 'No, please. I'm sorry. I had to do it. I had no choice. It was Father's legacy.' He felt dizzy and sick. A crushing pain in his chest made him gasp out loud. One minute, he was fighting for breath, then — nothing.

'What's happened?' asked Michael.

Sam felt for a pulse. 'No!' It was a howl of frustration. 'He can't be dead. This isn't how it was supposed to happen. We've waited years for this moment and the bastard has cheated us again.'

'Not really, Sam,' said Michael. 'He's just as dead as if I'd cut his throat, and it's less messy this way — no blood on our clothes. We'll untie him, then if he's found, they'll think he just staggered in here, got lost and died from the effort.' He stooped down to untie the binds that held Jolyon in place. 'Now we just need to put an end to his winery, and we're away on the next flight to Bangkok, freedom and a new life.'

Sam was reluctant to go, staring down at the bloated face and bulging eyes with raw hatred.

Michael tugged at her sleeve. 'Come on, leave him. We still have work to do.'

* * *

The events suite was empty of guests. Only the police and the catering staff remained. Sébastien and Marianne had returned from searching the house and winery for Jolyon and Suzy with no success.

'Where can they be?' asked Marianne, desperate. 'It's as if they've disappeared off the face of the earth.'

'People don't vanish in a puff of smoke, Mari,' said Sébastien. 'They have to be somewhere.' He was worried despite his bullish attitude.

'Are any of the cars missing, sir?' asked Jack.

'No, Inspector, it was one of the first things I checked. The keys are all there, too. Wherever they are, they went on foot.'

'It's a bit odd, in the middle of an important presentation,' said Bugsy, voicing what everyone was thinking.

Garwood appeared, looking irritable. 'What's going on here, Dawes? Mrs Garwood and I have been sitting here for over an hour listening to that godawful music and waiting for Richington-Blythe to get up on his hind legs and talk about his blasted wine. What's he up to?'

'I wish I could tell you, sir, but nobody seems to know. We can't find him.'

'I'm really worried,' said Marianne. 'It's his heart, you see. He's had a great deal of stress lately. People associated with the vineyard have been dying, including his own wife. Someone has been poisoning the vines. It's been too much. He could have collapsed at any time.'

'Well, we'd better find him,' said Garwood, mindful of his vote at the next lodge election. 'Call for backup, Dawes. I'm surprised you haven't done it already.'

Jack could imagine the aggravation Garwood would have given him if he had already done so. Complaints about manpower and budgets and making a fuss over nothing. 'Yes, sir. Very remiss of me, sir. I'll do it straight away.'

* * *

While they were waiting for the cavalry to arrive, Cynthia went to find Corrie and Carlene. 'Smashing food, Corrie. I didn't think much of the cabaret, though.'

'Cynthia, there wasn't a cabaret,' said Corrie, amused.

'Exactly. Why is everyone sprinting about looking glum?'

'They're looking for Jolyon. He's disappeared. Didn't George tell you?'

Cynthia shrugged. 'George never tells me anything. I expect Jolyon got fed up and went down the pub. I noticed a nice little country one in the main street, on the way here. It was called the Blythe Spirit. Clever name, don't you think?'

Corrie sighed. 'Cynthia, have you any idea at all what this evening was about?'

'Not really. George just said there'd be food, wine and a cabaret with a lot of French people. I was expecting the Can-Can, at least.'

Carlene attempted to explain. 'The "cabaret", Mrs Garwood, was meant to be Mr Richington-Blythe's sales pitch to a French wine conglomerate to save his vineyard, but he never turned up. Neither did the Wine Woman, to show the videos and organize the wine-tasting session at the end. The point is, the old man's got a dicky ticker and his daughter thinks he might have dropped dead somewhere inconvenient.'

'Well, shouldn't we be helping to look for him?' asked Cynthia.

'Sergeant Parsloe and his officers are on the way, but I guess we could have a stab at it,' agreed Corrie. 'Better than standing around here, doing nothing.'

'Let's split up,' suggested Carlene. 'We can use our phones to contact one another if we find anything.'

'Never mind the Old Bill!' exclaimed Cynthia, no longer bored. 'With the Three Cs on the case, we'll find him in no time. Let's get out there, ladies.'

* * *

It might have worked if Cynthia hadn't been accident-prone. She was poking about among the vines, looking for clues — she had no idea what — when she came upon a small circular structure, around three feet in diameter, with a pagoda-shaped roof. There was an opening on one side, and it occurred to her that, however unlikely, Jolyon might have staggered in there to rest until he was rescued. She crept inside to look and the ground suddenly fell away from under her feet. She plummeted some twenty feet down a hidden grape chute, and in the process, lost her phone, smashed her glasses and chipped a front tooth.

As for Corrie, she ignored Jack's behest ('Load up your catering van and go home, where you're safe, sweetheart. There really isn't anything useful for you to do here.') and set off to join the search, determined to prove him wrong. But instead of finding the missing person, she ended up becoming one herself. This left only Carlene, ever practical, to get the other Two Cs out of trouble.

CHAPTER TWENTY-TWO

From the inside, the grape chute looked rather like a curved chimney. It was an old structure, installed by the air commodore in 1954. Its purpose, during harvesting, had been to ensure the grapes had the shortest journey from vine to press, which was located in the winemaking cellar below. The chute was curved, so that the descent of the grapes would be slow, rather than a straight drop, which would have crushed them prematurely. Now it was something of an antiquity, and remained only for the curiosity of tourists. The mouth of the chute, protected from the elements by its small pagoda, was clearly visible in daylight, but at night, it was obscured in shadow.

Sitting on the stone floor in the dark, covered in dirt and cobwebs, Cynthia checked everything and decided she was intact, except for the broken tooth. *Damn!* she thought. *That crown was top-quality ceramic and cost George a fortune.* She reflected, somewhat uncharitably, that if Corrie had fallen in the blasted chimney instead of her, she'd just have stayed wedged in the top, being rather more generously proportioned than Cynthia. On a different occasion, it might have been quite exhilarating, like sliding down a white-knuckle flume at the water park. As it was, with her phone lost, she needed to find a way out, which wouldn't be easy with no light. And designer specs with trendy frames may look chic, but they weren't very functional with only the one remaining lens, which was cracked in several places.

* * *

Samantha and Michael emerged cautiously from the maze. 'Mikey, turn off your head torch. We don't want them to see us coming and anyway, I know my way around this place blindfolded.'

Parsloe and his uniformed officers had spread out and could be seen in the perimeter glare of the winery's outside lights, thrashing about in the undergrowth and searching the outbuildings.

'They'll have been told to look for an elderly man, possibly with a young woman,' said Sam. 'If they spot us, we'll tell them we're part of the presentation team helping with the search. Just follow my lead.'

With luck on their side, Sam and Michael reached their target unchallenged and scrambled down the flight of stone steps. Sam keyed the code into the security pad and watched it flash green. Then Michael hauled open the heavy, reinforced door and they hurried inside, closing it but without restoring the keypad security lock, so they could make a quick getaway. They were going to need it.

Sam turned on the lights, hoping they could not be seen from outside the cellar. She looked up at the massive stainless-steel tanks, standing high on their cylindrical legs, like serried ranks of knights in armour, mounting a crusade. A fanciful idea, maybe, but this was a crusade, of sorts.

'Won't they come looking for Jolyon in here?' asked Michael.

'I doubt it, and then only as a last resort. He's never been known to get involved in anything hands-on, not since his first wife died. He saw himself as the face of the Richington Vale brand. The menials did all the graft.'

Michael agreed. 'We never saw him in the village. Zack used to say it was beneath Jolyon to mix with the peasants. That's why he didn't recognize me in the maze.'

'Zack nearly saved us a job. They say he was on the point of beating Jolyon to death until that fat copper stopped him. Actually, the police have been pretty incompetent all round.'

'I thought the game was up when I caught old Potty Chambers giving me an old-fashioned look. You know the way she did, with her head on one side, as if trying to sum you up. I didn't think she would remember me from when I was seven, but I suppose it's possible.'

'That's why she had to die. It was only a matter of time before she recognized us both and put two and two together.'

Michael was anxious to finish the job and escape to safer climes. 'Can we get on with this? I don't think we should hang about. Where do we start?'

'Right down the far end, because once the wine starts to pour down out of those tanks, it'll flood this cellar very quickly, and we'll need to work our way towards the door so we can get out. I may like drinking wine, but I don't fancy drowning in it.'

Michael looked at the floor. 'Won't it run away through this grating?'

'Yes, but only slowly. It drains off into another cellar below. And in any case, it doesn't matter. Our objective, having hopefully damaged most of this year's vines, is to destroy the whole of last year's vintage, and put an end to Richington Vale Winery once and for all.'

They worked quickly. Starting on either side, they wrenched open the closing valves on each tank until the wine was gushing down in foaming streams, feeding the river that was beginning to swell beneath their feet.

* * *

Cynthia thought she could hear voices. She shouted up the chimney. 'Hello! Is anybody there? I'm Cynthia Garwood,

Chief Superintendent Garwood's wife. I'm trapped in this cellar and I can't get out. Can you tell George to send someone with a rope to haul me up, please?' She heard a dripping noise, then wine began to trickle through the cracked mortar in the wall — slowly, at first, but then gathering momentum, until Cynthia could feel it seeping into her Jimmy Choo sandals.

* * *

Corrie decided that if Jolyon had keeled over outdoors, Uniform would have found him by now. The maze never occurred to her — nor them — and she wouldn't have ventured inside it late at night, even if she'd thought of it. Her spatial memory was non-existent, even on a good day. It was due to a dodgy hippocampus, apparently. If she ever left a department store by a different door from the one she came in, she was totally disorientated, so mazes were out of the question.

Marianne had told her Jolyon was no longer an outdoors person, having spent too much of his life outside in all weathers, tending his precious vines. That meant he had to be somewhere under cover. She was fairly familiar with the layout of the kitchens and events suites, since she had catered there on many occasions. The police were searching all the rooms in the enormous house, waking the guests and asking them when they'd last seen Jolyon. They weren't popular. She turned off her phone. If either Cynthia or Carlene rang, it was bound to alert someone, and Jack would find out that she hadn't actually gone home. She would check it for missed calls from time to time.

All that remained were the buildings involved in the actual winemaking processes. She tried several, but the doors were securely locked, with the red security lights showing. She had no idea of the codes, so simply assumed, after briefly putting her ear to the doors, that there was no one inside. Added to which, it was really late now, and no workers were likely to be in there.

She was about to give up and return to the events suite to find out if Cynthia and Carlene had made any progress, when she came to the flight of stone steps leading down to the underground chamber of storage tanks. She stood at the top, looking at the heavy reinforced door, and could see a green light on the keypad. Someone must be inside.

* * *

'Carlene, have you seen Corrie and Mrs Garwood?' In situations like this, Jack became anxious when he couldn't actually see Corrie. She was an expert at disappearing and getting into danger, and there had been plenty of that around lately. 'The chief super has arranged a car to take Mrs Garwood home but he can't find her, and her phone is off. I thought Corrie had already left, but her green Coriander's Cuisine delivery van is still in the car park by the kitchens.'

Carlene and Antoine had mounted a joint search, checking the restaurant, café, canteens and even the walk-in freezers, in case Jolyon had staggered in there looking for help. 'Erm . . . no, Inspector Jack. I thought they were with you,' she lied. Better not say the Three Cs were back in action, 'helping' the police. It always prompted a rant about 'leaving the dangerous stuff to the experts' and 'look what happened the last time.'

'We'll have a squint around outside,' she promised. 'When we find them, we'll tell them you're looking for them.' Then, quietly, to Antoine, 'I've tried calling, but both their phones went straight to voicemail. I've got a funny feeling about this. Come on, quick.'

'*D'accord.*' Antoine had become familiar with Carlene's 'funny feelings'. He braced himself for trouble.

* * *

The wine was swirling around Cynthia's knees and rising. She'd had a brief notion that she would locate the source and block it up with some article of clothing. She was trying to work out what she would least like to sacrifice — the Louis Vuitton skirt or the Gucci blouse. She discarded this idea. As no useful light was penetrating from the mouth of the chimney, due to the curve, she had no way of seeing where the wine was coming in. In any event, the walls were so old, she guessed it would be filtering in from several places.

When the wine reached her knickers, she realized her situation was now serious and required a calm, carefully thought-out resolution. She began to scream.

* * *

Samantha and Michael had almost completed their mission. There were only a few tanks on each side left to open. The timing had been crucial. Even working as fast as they could, they were virtually swimming in wine, with each new gush sweeping them off their feet. Finally, they had to hold on to the closing valves and pull themselves up to the next tank, to avoid floating away.

'Isn't this enough?' Michael shouted. 'I think we should stop now and get out, while we can.'

'No,' Sam yelled back. 'We have to finish them all — for Mum and Dad.'

* * *

Carlene and Antoine were moving, unseen, among the rows of vines, when Carlene thought she heard faint screams.

'Ant, did you hear that?'

He shook his head. '*Non, cherie.* What is it that I am supposed to be hearing?'

'I thought I heard screaming.' She paused. 'There it is again. Listen.'

This time, Antoine heard it, too. They followed the sound to the mouth of the grape chute. Never one to employ caution at the expense of speed, Carlene blundered inside, and Antoine just managed to grab her in time to stop her from falling down the chimney.

'Bloody hell!' yelped Carlene, regaining her balance. 'That was close.' She stopped to listen again. 'Hang on. I was right. There's a woman down there, screaming.'

Antoine shone his flashlight down, but couldn't see anything. He was from Paris, the city that believes chivalry to be a totally French concept. He took a deep breath and made to slide down himself, but Carlene grabbed his arm. '*Ne sois pas andouille.* There has to be another way in.'

'How do you know?' Antoine never ceased to be impressed at Carlene's innate ability to work things out. It was one of the reasons he loved her.

'Because if this is what I think it is, they used to chuck grapes down it. Which means they had to get them back out again, after they'd been squashed into wine. I saw something similar at catering college, where they used to chuck bags of flour down, then make bread in the ovens in the cellar below. Either way, it would have involved some sort of transport of the finished product. We need to find a door to the cellar and there'll be some steps.'

* * *

The wine was up to Cynthia's bra. She was trying to think back to her schooldays and Old Droopy Draper's physics class. She wished she'd paid attention instead of painting her nails under the bench.

She couldn't see how much space there'd be between the final level of the wine and the ceiling of the cellar, and was trying to work out if there'd be sufficient air for her to swim up and take a breath. Probably not. She wondered if there was any kudos in drowning in wine rather than water. She'd taken a deep breath for one final scream, when a phone torch came on behind her and a familiar voice said, 'What are you doing sloshing about down there, Mrs Garwood?'

Cynthia breathed a huge sigh of relief, grateful it wasn't her last, as she'd feared. 'Carlene! Am I pleased to see you! How did you get in?'

'Through this door. If you'd paddled over this way a bit, you'd have found the steps leading up to it.'

Cynthia was livid. 'Do you mean I've been down here, slowly dissolving in Chardonnay, saying goodbye to George and preparing to die, when all I needed to do was climb up those steps and walk out the door?'

Antoine, ever the French *gentilhomme*, offered her his hand without smirking. 'This way, madame.'

'You'll be fine, now, Mrs Garwood,' assured Carlene. 'There's a police car waiting to take you home.' Secretly, she wondered what the driver would think of Chief Superintendent Garwood's wife sitting on the back seat, sopping wet and stinking of booze. But much more importantly, they needed to find Mrs D. Carlene still had that 'funny feeling' that she was in danger.

CHAPTER TWENTY-THREE

It was a few minutes short of midnight. Corrie couldn't imagine that anyone would be working in the storage chamber at that time, so there was every possibility that Jolyon could have stumbled in there and passed out. She had to check. He might still be alive.

Cautiously, she climbed down the steps. The door into the underground chamber was heavy, but as it wasn't securely locked, she reasoned that she should be able to pull it open. She had chef's arms, robust and muscular from kneading bread and lifting sacks of potatoes. She had several tries and eventually, after one immense heave, it gave way.

A tsunami of wine gushed out, pinning her backwards onto the stone steps and washing over her head. Taken completely by surprise, she gasped and spluttered, fighting for breath. There was nowhere for the wine to drain away, so it flooded the stairwell, rising ever higher. She thrashed about in it, trying to gain a foothold, but every time she found a step, she was washed off her feet by another wave.

She was choking now, trying to keep her head above the surface. Unable to swim, she gulped down several mouthfuls, her brain desperately trying to figure out a way to survive. Then, just as she was giving up — salvation. She saw them, splashing their way towards her from inside the chamber. She had no idea what they were doing in there, or why they were even together, but she didn't care. In that split second of recognition, she believed they would save her — the Wine Woman and the landlord of the Blythe Spirit.

'Suzy . . . Matt . . . help me!' She reached out, relieved and exhausted.

Sam grabbed her arms. Then she spun Corrie around, took her by the shoulders and forced her down, until her head was well under the wine. Michael struggled across to help his sister.

Desperate for oxygen, Corrie lost consciousness.

* * *

Once they had delivered Cynthia safely to the police car that would take her home for a hot bath and several restorative gins, Carlene and Antoine went in search of Corrie. Jack saw them go. He knew something was wrong and wanted to go with them, but Garwood was fussing about Jolyon, and how it would appear to Sir Barnaby if the entire Kings Richington Police Service had been unable to find one man on his own estate.

Jack appealed to Parsloe. 'Norman, can you keep an eye out for Mrs Dawes, please? Ask her to call me. Her phone is switched off and I keep getting voicemail. Nobody's telling me the truth, but I think she's gone missing, too.'

* * *

As soon as Corrie had pulled open the door, the bright lights inside the storage chamber had been clearly visible from some distance away. Carlene and Antoine saw them, and raced down the track that led to the storage chamber. At midnight, and given the circumstances, it was almost certainly criminal activity, but they had no notion exactly *how* criminal, until they arrived at the scene.

Carlene took in the situation immediately. Three figures were flailing about in an ocean of wine, and one of them, whom she recognized as Suzy Black, was holding Mrs D under. Without hesitation, and screaming as if the very hounds of hell were after her, she hurled herself from the top of the steps onto Suzy's back.

She hung on, grabbing her around the throat and squeezing hard, until Suzy was forced to let Corrie go or be strangled. Then Carlene grabbed a handful of Suzy's hair and pushed her under, with a strength she didn't know she possessed. That would teach her to try and drown her precious Mrs D!

As Matt reached out to try and help Suzy, Antoine recognized him from the occasions that he'd come to the events suite to fetch glasses on loan from the pub. He had never actually spoken to him, but he guessed this wasn't the time to extend a hand and say, 'How do you do?', according to the quaint British custom. He recalled instead a quaint French custom that, loosely translated, meant, 'Do unto others as they would do unto you — but do it first.' He punched Matt on the jaw, and with some satisfaction, watched him keel over backwards into the sea of wine.

Parsloe had spotted Carlene and Antoine sprinting in the direction of the lights and redirected his uniformed constables to the chamber. He phoned Jack, while he was still running. 'Jack, it's all kicking off at the wine storage. Carlene and Antoine are heading there, so I'm guessing Mrs Dawes is there, too. They may have found Richington-Blythe and Miss Black. We need to hurry.'

Seconds later, Jack and Bugsy appeared, followed by Aled and Gemma, breathless and hot on their heels. For a brief moment, they were speechless with disbelief at the scene before them. Uniformed constables were dragging who they believed to be Suzy Black and Matt Brown from the wine lake, dripping and half-conscious, like a couple of drowned rats. Then reality hit them, and Jack and Bugsy grabbed Corrie and pulled her out onto dry land.

She wasn't breathing.

Norman called for the emergency services, but Jack knew they wouldn't get there in time. He turned her onto her side and wine ran from her mouth, but she didn't take a breath. As far as he could tell, her heart wasn't beating and her face was ashen. Icy coldness clutched at the pit of his stomach.

Wet through and with a police blanket around her, Carlene was sobbing uncontrollably in Antoine's arms. As a toddler, she'd been yanked away from her biological mother's skirts and had grown up, unhappily, in various care homes. Corrie was the only real mother figure she'd ever known, and she loved her. To lose her was unthinkable.

Bugsy was shaken but still had his wits about him. 'CPR, Jack. We have to try, and quickly.' Then, when Jack didn't respond, 'Do you want me to do it?'

Unable to speak and trying desperately to remember his training, Jack lay Corrie on her back, tilted her head gently and lifted her chin. He pinched her nose, put his mouth over hers and blew steadily, watching for her chest to rise. He performed another rescue breath, then thirty chest compressions. Still, she didn't breathe.

By now, they were surrounded by uniformed coppers, stunned and praying for a miracle. Bugsy was silent for once but ready to take over, if Jack needed a rest. Jack performed the routine six times without a response. Unable to even contemplate a life that didn't have his funny, feisty, wonderful wife in it, he cried out in anguish, 'Corrie, my darling, please breathe. Please say something.'

Corrie opened her eyes and took a long, shuddering breath. Then she said, 'I never want another glass of Chardonnay as long as I live.'

* * *

Suzy Black and Matt Brown were bundled into separate ambulances to be checked out in hospital. On release, they'd be cautioned and arrested on suspicion of the attempted murder of Corrie Dawes. While the MIT was not yet aware of any other crimes, Jack didn't believe that trying to drown Corrie would turn out to be the only one — but it was the one that made him determined to get them the longest sentence possible. His copper's nose told him that some incisive questioning would reveal more, including the whereabouts of Jolyon Richington-Blythe.

At one point, Garwood had tried to take Dawes off the case, thinking he was too involved personally. Jack was having none of it. He pointed out that they still hadn't found Jolyon, and it would take time to bring another SIO up to speed. He was, he argued, by far the best officer to bring these two to justice and find Jolyon — alive or dead. Garwood saw his point and allowed him to continue, with a warning not to overstep the mark while interrogating the woman.

'What does he think I'm going to do, Bugsy, jump over the desk and throttle her?'

Bugsy was honest. 'It's what I'd want to do, if she'd harmed my Iris.' He hesitated. 'Corrie is OK, isn't she, Jack? I know she's tough, but that was a terrifying experience for anybody.'

Jack frowned. 'She says she is, but you know Corrie. If she had two broken legs and an arm hanging off, she'd still be in her kitchen, whipping up a soufflé with the good arm. Carlene is hovering around her like Florence Nightingale. She's promised to ring me if she's at all worried.'

* * *

While Suzy and Matt were in hospital and vulnerable, they had admitted to being brother and sister, and had asked to be treated together. It was made clear to the doctors that they should be kept apart. Two uniformed constables were assigned to ensure that happened. After they were brought from the hospital to the station, they were put in separate cells, then separate interview rooms. There was no way they were going to be allowed to compare notes and cook up a cock-and-bull story of total innocence.

Jack was determined that he would question Suzy, guessing she would be the toughest nut to crack, but most of all, he needed to know *why*. There had to be a rational reason why a seemingly sane, intelligent woman and her pleasant, hard-working brother would try to murder Corrie.

Bugsy opted to interview Matt Brown, with Aled riding shotgun. Aled was finding it equally hard to connect this suspect with the amiable young man who had served him and Gemma in the Blythe Spirit that day. It just proved that dangerous people come in many disguises, sometimes even as friends.

Jack took Gemma in with him to work the digital recording. It was vital to get it right, as it would be presented as evidence in court when the charges proceeded to trial, as he was determined they should. He postponed questions about the attempted murder of his wife and used shock tactics to unsettle her. He went straight for the jugular. 'What have you done with Jolyon Richington-Blythe, Miss Black? Did you kill him?'

She blinked at his directness. 'The individual human response to an accusation like that, Inspector, is often a state of denial, minimization or externalization. In my case, it's all three. Make of that what you will.'

Suzy had opted for the duty solicitor as she didn't feel that Peter Leggett would be particularly sympathetic, given the accusations she was facing. The duty solicitor reminded Jack that this was not a fishing trip and Miss Black was here to answer questions about an attempted murder, which she strongly denied.

She'd been issued with a white tracksuit. The blue paper boiler suits, originally deployed by the police in these situations, could no longer be used in case they 'infringed the suspect's human rights'. Her own clothes had been taken away for forensic examination, although Jack doubted whether they'd find anything useful, since they were soaked in Chardonnay. Her auburn hair, no longer in a neat, shiny pleat, hung about her shoulders in bedraggled ringlets.

Following best-practice guidelines, insisted on by Chief Superintendent Garwood, she'd been told that an officer or family member could be sent to Richington Hall, to fetch some items of her clothing, if that's what she would prefer. She had laughed aloud at that, thinking neither Sébastien nor Marianne would be disposed towards making her feel more comfortable, and her only relative was in the next interview room.

Jack came to the point. 'Can you explain why you were attempting to drown Mrs Coriander Dawes when you were arrested?'

'I was doing nothing of the kind. She had fallen into the deepest part of the wine outflow and obviously couldn't swim. I was doing my best to rescue her when that lunatic girl jumped on me. I was the one who nearly drowned. Then that half-witted foreigner punched my brother, who had been coming to help us, and next thing I knew, your woodentops turned up and dragged us away. It was a fiasco of monumental proportions. You couldn't make it up.'

'Are you denying that you and Matt Brown, the man we now know to be your brother, deliberately opened all the wine tanks, flooding the cellar and beyond?'

'Of course I'm denying it. Why would we do that? Jolyon employs me as his Master of Wine and his son has asked me to marry him. I'll soon be part of the family. Matt has been managing the Richington-Blythes' pub very successfully with his partner, Freddy. What possible reason would we have for trying to ruin Jolyon? Someone else sabotaged those tanks and we had just gone to see if we could save any of the wine. You have all this completely wrong, Inspector.' She sighed theatrically. 'I'd like to take a break now. May I speak to my brother?'

'No, I'm afraid not.' Jack stood up. 'I'll have some tea sent in. For the record, Inspector Dawes and Constable Fox are leaving the room.'

Next door, Bugsy wasn't having much success either. Matt answered every question with 'No comment,' despite being told he wasn't helping himself by not cooperating. He asked, several times, if he could speak to his sister. On being told he could not, he became truculent. 'Either charge me or let me go.'

Because both siblings were suspected of attempted murder, Jack applied for an extension of the customary twenty-four hours to ninety-six. It was approved. He had just under four days to charge them, or he would have to let them go.

CHAPTER TWENTY-FOUR

'Are you sure you're well enough to go back to work, Corrie?'
Jack had so nearly lost the love of his life, he was terrified to
let her out of his sight.

'Of course I am,' she insisted. 'Carlene and I have a full
order book. I can't leave it all to her and the team.'

'You should have seen her, Corrie. She fought that
woman like a wildcat to stop her from drowning you.'

'I know.' Corrie paused, thinking how very fond she
and Carlene were of each other, although they didn't always
say it. 'I'd have no ill effects at all, if it hadn't been for some
great oaf jumping up and down on my chest. My ribs are
really painful.'

'Sorry,' said Jack.

She put her arms around him. 'Don't be.' She was curious. 'Has the Wine Woman told you why she was trying to
kill me?'

'No. Just the opposite. She says you were drowning, and
she was actually trying to save you when Carlene jumped on
her.'

'That's nonsense. I reached out to her and she grabbed
me and held me under. I'd be a goner if it weren't for Carlene
— and you, of course, sweetheart.'

'But why? That's what I can't work out. What have you ever done to her?'

Corrie furrowed her brows in thought. 'I don't think it was because of anything I'd done, it was because of what I'd seen. Suzy and Matt were coming out of the storage chamber together, having sabotaged the wine. They didn't want any witnesses to that, did they?'

Jack's mind went back to the murders of Patricia Chambers and Robbie McKendrick. The team had previously decided that the reason they were killed wasn't because of something they'd done, but because of something they'd seen. That was why they hadn't had an anonymous letter beforehand, accusing them. It had been spontaneous, not premeditated. Like the attempted murder of his wife. 'Corrie, you're brilliant. I think I'm finally starting to understand.'

'Good. Do you fancy seabass for supper? It'll feed your little grey cells.'

* * *

Back in the incident room, Jack went across to Clive. 'Were the two suspects fingerprinted when they were arrested?'

'Absolutely, sir. And a DNA sample taken.'

'Can we run them through the database?'

'You bet, sir. Give me five minutes.'

'Are you thinking they might have previous, guv?' asked Bugsy.

'They only turned up in Richington Vale around three years ago, so nobody knows much about them. It certainly wasn't common knowledge that they were brother and sister. Why do you suppose they kept that quiet, until now? You'd think unmarried siblings living in the same village would at least socialize together, like Sheila and Miles Barton.'

'Maybe they weren't very close,' offered Gemma. 'I've got an older sister and we don't get on at all. She's very much the "little woman", straight out of a 1950s *How to Be the Perfect Wife* handbook. She's only one brain cell short of putting ribbons in her hair, for when her husband comes home from work to his delicious dinner and warm slippers. She gave up a good career to have four children in rapid succession.'

'I can see how you wouldn't have much in common,' said Bugsy, winking at Aled, who knew when to keep his mouth shut.

Clive returned, clutching a printout. 'This is interesting, sir. The brother has form. Got into bad company as an adolescent. After a spate of burglaries, he graduated to stealing cars. He did several stretches in a young offender institution in Newcastle, until the magistrate finally got fed up with giving him the benefit of the doubt and sent him down for two years. When he came out, he bought a gun and held up a post office. He got another sentence that ended three years ago, just before he came to Richington Vale. It was in the nick that he met Freddy Marshall, the hotpot king, listed on his record sheet as a known associate.'

'How did he get a personal licence for the Blythe Spirit with a criminal record?' asked Aled.

'He didn't disclose it. And in any case, Matt Brown isn't his real name. It's Michael Baker. And his sister's name is Samantha Baker.'

'Blimey,' said Bugsy. 'And does she have a criminal record, too?'

'Yep,' said Clive. 'Shoplifting and forgery. But what she *doesn't* have is a Master of Wine qualification. I checked with the Institute. Not in either name — Suzy Black or Samantha Baker.'

'It looks like Jolyon Richington-Blythe took them both at face value and gave them each a job,' said Jack. 'They're both fakes.'

'That's what happens when you consider yourself too important to follow the correct procedures,' said Gemma piously.

'Just out of curiosity, I checked the records of the local primary school,' said Clive. 'They go back donkey's years. A couple of kids called Sam and Mikey Baker attended there until around twenty years ago, then they dropped off the radar, aged ten and seven.'

'I thought I recognized those two kiddies on the school photo,' recalled Jack triumphantly. 'Do you remember, Bugsy? The two coppernobs on the end? I bet that was them.'

'It's a pity the old headmistress isn't still alive,' said Bugsy. 'I bet Potty Chambers would have remembered them.'

'That, Sarge,' observed Aled, 'is almost certainly why she *isn't* still alive. Because she did remember them. If she spoke to Samantha Baker, aka Suzy Black, at the *Echo* charity event and said something along the lines of, "Don't I know you from somewhere?", it would have sealed her fate. She couldn't be allowed to leave alive. And who better than Suzy Black to have free access to the polyurethane gloves used by the vine workers, and the hydrogen cyanide insecticide found in the flask.'

'That's pure evil,' said Gemma.

'They are evil,' agreed Jack. 'Both of them. And now I believe we have enough to unnerve them, but we'll have to play it cool.'

'Do you reckon they'll cough up to the murders of Anstruther, Beacham and McKendrick, sir?' asked Mitch. He was still feeling bad about Sandra Richington-Blythe hiding from him in the grape hopper.

'I hope so, once they know we're on to them. But we need them to tell us what they've done with Jolyon. It could be he's still alive.'

'I very much doubt it, guv,' said Bugsy. 'I think he was the target for their whole venture. All the other deaths were either leading up to it, or collateral damage. I shouldn't be surprised if he was already dead before they flooded his wine cellar.'

* * *

The countdown had begun. There were only two and a half days left to gather actual proof of guilt or a confession. So far, all they had was the failure to disclose a criminal record and obtaining a job using false qualifications. Everything else was circumstantial. You couldn't convict on a multiple murder charge on the grounds that it was most likely that they'd done it.

It was becoming increasingly obvious that neither Samantha nor Michael intended to give anything away under interrogation. Samantha had openly stated that she and her brother were innocent of any crimes and would simply sit it out until Jack was forced to let them go. Then they would find a good solicitor, sue the police for wrongful arrest and Carlene and Antoine for assault.

Early the next morning, they were brought from their cells for more questions. Fed up with pussyfooting around, Jack came straight to the point. 'What can you tell me about the murders of Bob Beacham, James Anstruther, Patricia Chambers and Robbie McKendrick?'

She didn't turn a hair. 'Absolutely nothing. Except I would suggest that your Murder Investigation Team isn't making good use of taxpayers' money if you have four unsolved murders on your hands.'

Jack decided it was time he told her that he was aware of the false names and criminal records. 'Why have you been using different names since you came to live in Richington Vale?'

She leaned across to whisper in her solicitor's ear and he nodded. 'I don't believe there's a law against using any names we like,' she said, 'as long as it isn't for fraudulent purposes. It's true we have criminal records, but those convictions have been spent. We were making a fresh start when we came here to work three years ago, so we thought we'd take fresh names. Nothing sinister in that.'

'But you used them to obtain advantage — your job as a Master of Wine, which you aren't, and your brother's job as a licensee, having failed to disclose a criminal record.'

'Minor deceptions in the scheme of things, Inspector, compared to the murders you're trying to pin on us.'

And so they continued with their game of cat and mouse until it was close to the time when Jack had to end the interview for the day. That meant only one more day to crack them.

'When did you last see Mr Richington-Blythe?' he asked.

'I really can't remember. He was supposed to be presenting my brilliantly constructed presentation, "The Richington Vale World of Wine", but he never turned up. If he's a missing person, I believe it's the police's job to find him, Inspector. I don't believe the onus is on me to help you. And if you're as good at finding people as you are at solving murders, I don't give much for Jolyon's chances.'

* * *

Jack was exhausted from sheer nervous energy when he got home. He didn't think there was much left in the criminal world to surprise him, but those two certainly had. He appealed to Corrie. 'Who'd have thought elegant, clever Suzy Black would turn out to be scheming Samantha Baker, and Matt "everybody likes him" Brown is actually murdering Mikey Baker?'

'They both kept the same initials,' she said. 'Isn't that's a bit weird?'

'Not really. It's quite common when people have several aliases. My job now is to prove to the satisfaction of the CPS that they carried out four murders. And when we find Jolyon, it could turn out to be five.'

'Blimey, that's awful.' Corrie bit her lip. 'Do you think you'll do it?'

'It's either that or shoehorn a confession out of them, which at the moment, is looking very unlikely.'

'I don't understand why they came back after twenty years and used false names to kill people. They could have done it equally well using their own names.'

'It would have been risky. These weren't random killings — well, not all of them. They were on a mission and we don't yet know what that was. If they'd kept their old names, someone here might have remembered them, picked up on a connection and put a stop to it. What they wanted was to complete their quest, then disappear back into anonymity. The problem is, they've very nearly achieved exactly that. I've got to get them, Corrie, if only for what they tried to do to you.'

* * *

Back at Richington Hall, Sébastien and Marianne were still in shock from current events, not least because their father still hadn't been found. Marianne especially was confused and upset. Richington Vale was rife with rumours. The gossips got hold of a titbit of information and made up the rest to suit themselves. 'Seb, where has Papa gone?'

Sébastien passed a weary hand across his brow. His world, which only days ago had seemed full of hope and potential, had collapsed at his feet. A new job, in a new country, with a new wife wasn't going to happen, especially now his intended fiancée was in custody at the police station. She and her brother were suspected of all manner of crimes, if the scandalmongers were to be believed.

'I don't know, Mari. Father has pulled a few crazy stunts in the past in the interests of the winery, but I can't see any reason for a disappearing act.' Seb feared the worst. Something told him his father was lying dead somewhere, but the police had searched every inch of the place, with no success. 'I believe the next step is to search with a police helicopter.'

'Search for his body, you mean?'

Seb didn't answer.

'Why have the police arrested Suzy and Matt? I don't understand.'

'Mari, people are saying that those aren't their real names.'

'But why would they call themselves something different?'

Seb sighed. 'When people use false names, it's usually because they want to hide something or commit a crime. The police think that in this case it's both.'

Marianne was silent for a while, thinking. 'Seb, there was something strange about Suzy Black, or whatever her real name is. Do you remember when she was mugged and you brought her to live here, at the Hall?'

'What about it?'

'She said that what really upset her was that the mugger had stolen her Hermès handbag. It was the sapphire blue one and very expensive. But when she unpacked her clothes, she still had it. I thought she must have been mistaken from the blow to her head, but now I am thinking it's rather peculiar.'

'Yes, very peculiar,' agreed Seb.

'Now that she's been arrested, do you think I should mention it to Inspector Dawes?'

Sébastien's utopian future was in tatters now. It could hardly make things worse. 'Yes, I think perhaps you should.'

CHAPTER TWENTY-FIVE

The breakthrough, when it came, was from two most unexpected sources. The Blythe Spirit, hub of the village community, was buzzing with gossip about the disappearance of Jolyon, self-styled Lord of the Manor. With Matt, the landlord, in police custody, Zack and Rosie were making a good job of keeping the pub running, despite being bombarded with questions, to which they had no answers.

'Where's old Richington-Blythe gone, Zack? Is it true they think he killed your mum then legged it, after you beat him up?' asked someone with all the sensitivity of a charging rhino.

'No, that's not right,' someone else contradicted. 'They're saying our Matt stuck a knife in Robbie McKendrick. Never liked him, anyway. I haven't forgotten that fight he had with the vicar.'

'That's rubbish,' said the woman from two doors down who came in to play the piano. 'Why would Matt do that? He's a lovely young man. Everyone likes Matt.'

Even old Dave put in his twopenn'orth. 'It's my belief that it's the wine-tasting woman what's causing all the trouble. Haven't I always said she's a swanky piece of work? Who's in the chair, Rosie, love? I'm parched.'

'Sorry to interrupt,' said Miles Barton, tentatively, 'but are our hotpots ready? Sheila and I ordered half an hour ago. Normally, I wouldn't hassle Freddy, but we've got a fundraising meeting with the vicar about his plans for the new boxing club.'

'Sorry, Miles,' said Zack. 'I'll go and check.' In the kitchen, Zack couldn't see any sign of cooked hotpots. Freddy was hunched over his oven, with tears streaming down his face.

Zack put an arm around his shoulders. 'Whatever's the matter, mate? I know you must be missing Matt, but it'll be all right. Don't listen to all the gossip. The police will realize he's innocent and let him go, you'll see.'

'But that's just it,' wept Freddy. 'I'm not sure he is innocent, and I can't keep quiet any longer. Too many people have died. I have to tell the police what I know, even though it breaks my heart.'

* * *

There was quite a turnout in the village hall for the boxing club fundraising initiative, which they were calling 'Pounds for Punches'. The vicar was seated at a table at the front, with the secretary on one side and the treasurer on the other. On the wall behind him, the seemingly mandatory fundraising thermometer showed how much had been collected so far. It was difficult to see at first glance, because the hall was also used by the mothers and toddlers' group, and some of them had scribbled on it with crayons, so it could have been five hundred pounds or a wiggly worm and two smiley faces.

'Good evening, everyone.' The vicar beamed. 'May I say how rewarding it is to see so many friends willing to give up their time to raise money for the new boxing club. Plans for restoring the old Richington Vale children's home on the outskirts of the village are advancing well. I have been to look at the building, and over the years, it has fallen into disrepair. It will cost a good deal to transform it into the modern-day boxing gym our young people deserve.'

A lady in a putty-coloured cardigan stood up. 'Vicar, are you able to confirm, categorically, that there'll be no posters of snarling boxing legends on the walls, or obscene graffiti in the changing rooms — and no spitting. Otherwise, I am unable to commit to Tarquin joining. He's very impressionable.'

The lady next to her nodded in agreement. 'My Julian bruises easily — I shouldn't want him to get hit in the face.'

A muscular young lady in training gear took out her chewing gum to ask, 'Will girls be able to join?'

'Absolutely, Tracy. Everyone will be welcome. How is the T-shirt project going, Emma?'

She stood up. 'Slowly, Reverend. There was a difference of opinion over the slogan. Some of the committee liked "Spare a nicker for the vicar", but on the grounds that some of the younger people didn't know that a "nicker" was another word for a pound, and thought it referred to ladies' undergarments, we opted for the second one. However, there's still some controversy. While the striking graphics of purses and wallets get the fundraising message across, some of the older ladies were reluctant to have "Don't delay — get yours out today" displayed on their bosoms.'

'Er . . . yes . . . very good. Well done, ladies. The Pledge Challenge is going well. The ladies' bungee jumping team obtained magnificent sponsorship, which amounted to five pounds a rebound. Local businesses have responded splendidly to the call, and I'm happy to say that the Blythe Spirit is donating fifty pence for every hotpot sold. Sheila and Miles Barton from the Flower Pot are offering a beautiful bouquet as a raffle prize, so get selling those tickets, everyone.'

On their way home, Sheila and Miles were unusually quiet.

Miles broke the silence. 'Should we feel guilty that the vicar is never going to get his boxing club?'

'No, certainly not. I understand his concern for the youngsters of the village, and it's true there's very little for them to do but hang about in gangs looking for mischief, but we have to finish what we started. It might have been many years ago, but to me, it seems like only yesterday.'

'Yes. Me too.'

* * *

Next morning, aware that he had only twenty-four hours before he had to release the Bakers, Jack was preparing to question Samantha, and this time he intended to be tough.

Just as he was about to ask for her to be brought from her cell to the interview room, Sergeant Parsloe phoned. 'Jack, I've got Freddy Marshall on the desk, asking to speak to you. He says it's urgent.'

'OK, Norman. Send him up.' Sam Baker could wait. 'Bugsy, you're with me. Gemma can sit in and make notes, in case we miss something.'

'What do you reckon he wants, guv?' asked Bugsy.

'Clive, remind me what we know about Freddy Marshall.'

Clive scrolled through his laptop. 'He was Michael Baker's cellmate during his last stretch in the nick. Baker was in for armed robbery. Marshall got two years for being found in possession of an article with a blade in a public place without good reason or lawful authority. He maintained that although he worked as a hairdresser, he wanted to be a chef and it was his vegetable knife, but the beak didn't believe him. During his spell inside, he worked in the kitchens and gained qualifications as a chef.'

'That's a bit harsh,' said Gemma. 'He obviously had an interest in cooking, so maybe it really was his vegetable knife.'

'They're very tough on knife crime,' said Clive. 'There had been a few incidents of stabbings in the tower block where he lived. Maybe they wanted to make him an example.'

'Let's see what he has to tell us,' said Jack.

* * *

Having been sent down once already, Freddy was naturally cautious. He looked around nervously at Bugsy and Gemma.

'It's about Mikey,' he began. 'There's something you need to know.'

'OK, Mr Marshall,' said Jack. 'Don't worry about the other officers here. Just tell me, in your own words.'

'It was the night of the pub quiz, when Doctor Anstruther got run over and killed. The police questioned everybody in the pub about where they were when it happened.' He paused to sip the tea that Constable Johnson had brought him. 'You know that Mikey and I were in prison together?'

'Yes, we do, sir.'

'I always knew he had a tendency to violence, but when we came here, he said he'd turned over a new leaf. He'd changed his name and it was the start of our new life together. He said I was never to call him Mikey. His name was Matt now.'

'Did he ever mention Samantha Baker?' asked Bugsy.

'No. I was as surprised as everyone else when it turned out Suzy Black was his sister. Obviously, I haven't had a chance to speak to him about it.'

Rumours evidently did travel fast in this village. 'Go on, Mr Marshall.'

'The police asked Mikey if he'd heard anything of the accident. He said no, he'd been down in the cellar changing a barrel, ready for the next day, and only came up when he heard the commotion. Well, that wasn't true. I'd gone down there earlier to ask him if I could increase the meat order from the butcher, and he wasn't there.'

'But wouldn't you have seen him, if he'd come back up?' Bugsy wanted to know.

'No. There's a door from the cellar and some steps leading up to where we keep our cars. I wondered where he'd gone, so I went to look.' He gulped. 'Mikey's car wasn't there. Then everything kicked off in the bar, and a few minutes later, Mikey reappeared.'

Jack paused for a moment. 'Are you telling us that you think Michael Baker ran Doctor Anstruther down?'

'I know he did. Later that night, I couldn't sleep. I sneaked out to look at his car. It had a badly dented wing and there was

. . . blood. Early next morning, before I was up, he took it to a body repair shop out of town and got it repaired. I saw the bill in his wallet. He must have told them he hit an animal.'

'Why did you leave it until now to tell us this, Mr Marshall?'

'Because he's my partner and I love him. Everybody loves Mikey. But when all the other terrible things started happening to people — Miss Chambers, Mr McKendrick and Zack's mother — he became short-tempered, uncommunicative, as if he was working up to something really bad. He started talking in his sleep about how he'd put an end to them all, especially Jolyon. When there was trouble up at the winery and you arrested him and his sister, I knew I had to speak out.'

'You realize you could be charged with withholding evidence, Mr Marshall?'

He sighed, as if glad to have got it off his chest. 'I know, Inspector. I told myself it wasn't as bad as I thought, but it is, isn't it?'

'I fear so, but you've done the right thing. Thank you for coming in.'

'I feel dreadful about grassing him up. It's the worst thing you can do to someone you care about.'

'Don't feel too badly,' said Bugsy. 'When we searched him, we found two plane tickets to Bangkok. He planned to leave straight after he'd sabotaged the wine.'

Tears rolled down Freddy's cheeks. 'Mikey was taking me to Bangkok?'

'No, sir. The tickets were in the names of Michael and Samantha Baker. He was escaping justice with his sister.'

* * *

Jack was about to summon Samantha for the second time, when his phone rang again.

'You're popular today, Jack,' said Parsloe. 'I've got Miss Marianne Richington-Blythe to see you. She says it might be nothing, but she thinks she should speak to you anyway.'

'OK, Norman. Ask her to come up.'

Marianne was a little pale and had lost weight over the past weeks, but otherwise she was perfectly calm and composed. She wore a pale blue dress and jacket with a silk scarf, tied casually about her shoulders, and was carrying a large tote bag. Gemma was impressed by how cool and classy French ladies seemed to remain, when all about them are hot and dishevelled. But she wasn't sure about the tote bag. It didn't seem to go with the outfit.

She came straight to the point. 'I need to talk to you about a handbag, Inspector.' Her French accent was more pronounced when she was unsure of herself.

'A handbag?' repeated Jack, channelling Lady Bracknell. 'I see.' But he didn't see. What possible relevance could a handbag have, when he had murders to solve. 'Are we talking about any particular handbag, miss?'

'*Bien sûr*. It is an Hermès handbag, sapphire blue.'

Gordon Bennett! thought Gemma. *If she's come to report it missing, I hope she had it insured.*

'It was the one Suzy was carrying, the night she was mugged. She was upset, she said, because the mugger ran off with it. But that can't be right, Inspector, because she still has it. Look.' She opened the tote and pulled out the blue handbag. 'I took it from her room, after she was arrested. It still contains all the things she claimed the mugger had stolen from her. I thought you should know.'

Jack passed it to Gemma and she looked inside, thinking this was as close as she'd ever get to a bag like this. 'It's all here, sir.'

'*Eh bien*, why would Suzy pretend to have been robbed?' asked Marianne.

'I don't know, miss, but I intend to find out. We'll keep the bag for now, if you don't mind. Constable Fox will give you a receipt.'

As she was leaving, Marianne turned back. 'Suzy isn't the lady we thought she was, is she? Sébastien says it isn't even her real name. Can you tell me what she has done, Inspector?'

'I'm afraid not. But I'm sure it will all become clear very soon.' *Especially*, he thought, *with the intel we've received this morning.*

CHAPTER TWENTY-SIX

It was with renewed vigour that Dawes approached the interview with Samantha Baker. Gemma took the handbag in,
concealed in a large evidence bag.

Samantha smiled confidently and looked at the clock on
the wall. 'You're late today, Inspector. Now you only have
about eight hours before my brother and I walk out of here.'

Jack smiled back. 'Before you go, Miss Baker, I wonder
if you'd mind taking me through what happened to you the
night you were mugged.'

She pulled a face. 'Must I? You surely have my statement
somewhere. Can't you refer to that? It was a very upsetting
experience and one I don't care to relive.'

'As you wish.' Jack turned to Gemma. 'DC Fox, I believe
you have a record of Miss Baker's account of the incident.
Would you mind reading it out, please?'

Gemma pulled it up on her laptop and began to read.
When she came to the part where Samantha had said the
mugger had snatched her bag and ran off with it, Jack asked,
'Could you describe the bag, Miss Baker?'

'Yes. It was an Hermès — sapphire blue. Very expensive,
not that you would know anything about that.' She gave

Gemma a patronizing look. 'I dare say it has been sold on the black market by now.'

'Would you recognize it, if you saw it again?'

'Yes, of course. But I'm not likely to, am I?'

Jack nodded to Gemma, who reached down and pulled it from the evidence bag. She held it up. 'Is that it?' Jack asked.

Samantha looked bewildered now, unsure what to say. 'Er . . . yes, I think so. Where did you find it?'

'Surprisingly enough, Miss Richington-Blythe brought it in. She found it in your room at Richington Hall. It still has all your possessions in it, the ones you declared stolen, in your statement.'

She reached out to snatch it, but Gemma whipped it away. 'In that case, she must have got it from the man who mugged me.' She made a last desperate effort. 'It must have been Sébastien. Yes, that's it. They're in it together. Don't you see? They wanted to sell the vineyard, but Jolyon wouldn't agree, so they got rid of him and now they're trying to implicate me and my brother.'

'The game's up, Miss Baker. You weren't mugged at all, were you? Your brother beat you up.'

'That's ridiculous. Why would Mikey do that?'

'To divert suspicion away from you, after you poisoned Miss Chambers. She recognized you at the charity event, didn't she? You had to get rid of her before she remembered who you were, and then it wouldn't have taken her long to connect you to your brother. She had already written about him in her journal. From there, it was only a matter of time before she reported her suspicions to the police, and the whole deception would have unravelled.'

She looked about her, as if for an escape. Then, sensing her brother was next door, she stood up and screamed, 'Don't say anything, Mikey!'

It was too late. In the adjacent interview room, Bugsy was telling Michael Baker about Freddy Marshall's evidence.

'No point lying anymore, Mr Baker. We know it was you who ran over Doctor Anstruther. We have impounded your car and it's with our forensics team. I know you had it repaired, but if there's even the tiniest drop of blood on it — and there will be — you can be certain they will find it and match it to the doctor. Do you want to tell me why you killed him?'

'I don't believe you. Freddy would never grass. We were cellmates together.'

'We know that, but Mr Marshall has a streak of decency and couldn't keep quiet about what he knew. He also claims that you murdered Beacham and McKendrick. Apparently, you mutter about it in your sleep. Now that we know, we'll get a warrant and turn over your flat and the pub. Of course, we won't find the pruning knife that you stuck into Mr McKendrick, because you left it in his chest, but there'll be several other incriminating items with your fingerprints. Why don't you tell us the whole story?'

Baker sank down in his chair. No longer defiant, he seemed small and crushed. 'You must understand, what we did wasn't random, with no purpose. It was carefully planned, over a very long time. My father, Thomas Baker, worked here for twenty-five years. He was a good employee and worked his way up to vineyard manager. Then, he got sick.

'Everyone knew it was because of the pesticides that he'd absorbed, every day, out in the fields, but when he died, Doctor Anstruther said it was because he chain-smoked and the tar and nicotine had destroyed his lungs. Richington-Blythe wouldn't give my mother any compensation and turned us out of our cottage.

'Mother had no choice but to take us to live with our grandparents, who weren't well themselves. She worked in a supermarket by day and cleaned offices at night, in addition to caring for her parents.' He paused, head in his hands.

'After living in a village in the country, going to the local primary school, Sam and I found city life hard and hostile. With no father, and a mother always working, we got into trouble. Then Mum died. We made a pact that one day, we'd punish Richington-Blythe and the others. Beacham, who'd been after Dad's job and confirmed that he smoked all the time, and, of course, Anstruther. We took different names, came here to live, and after three years of settling into the community, it was the right time to carry out our mission. I began by poisoning the vines. As for McKendrick and Potty Chambers, they were in the wrong place at the wrong time and had to be eliminated, so that we'd be free to put an end to Jolyon. It was a shame, but nothing was going to stop us. The rest you know.'

'What about trying to drown Mrs Dawes? How did that fit in? She hadn't done you any harm.'

'No, but she saw us coming out of the storage chamber, after we'd released the wine. She would have identified us. We couldn't let her live. As it was, that mad girl jumping on Sam and her boyfriend knocking me out ruined everything. We knew once you had our prints, you'd trace us from our criminal records.'

'One thing I don't understand, Mr Baker. What was the point of the anonymous letters?'

His smile was half-hearted. 'It was just another ploy to divert attention away from us. Everyone who knew Matt Brown and Suzy Black knew they didn't believe in God. We never showed up in church or at any of the vicar's community projects, like the other villagers. It was unlikely we would quote the Bible. But we wanted Beacham, Anstruther and Jolyon to know they were being threatened, that somebody knew what they'd done. There's nothing like a fierce tract from the Bible to put the wind up the superstitious.'

It was then that they heard Samantha scream the warning.

Mikey shouted back in despair, 'It's all over, Sam. They've got us.'

Bugsy spoke gently. 'Do yourself a favour, son. Tell us what you've done with Jolyon Richington-Blythe.'

'Never! He's the reason we did any of this. He can rot in hell.'

They were charged with four counts of murder and murder by joint enterprise. The CPS supported the charges. But it wasn't over — not entirely. While Jack was certain they had killed Jolyon, neither of them would reveal the whereabouts of the body, and without one, conviction for his murder would prove much more difficult.

* * *

Police Constable Fiona Wainwright paid a final visit to Barbara Beacham to tell her that someone had been charged with Bob's murder, and she would soon be able to have his body for a funeral.

'Matt Brown?' Barbara repeated, unconvinced. 'The landlord of the Blythe Spirit? It can't be. Why would he want to kill my Bob?'

'I haven't got all the details, Barbara, but it was to do with something that happened twenty years ago at the vineyard. Bob took on the job of a man called Thomas Baker, when he became ill and died. It was a promotion, apparently.'

'Yes, I remember. It was quite a lot more money and we needed it because the children were still young. Management persuaded Bob to say that Thomas got ill from smoking, when Bob knew it was from the pesticides.'

'The man who's been charged with killing Bob was Thomas's son.'

'And he was the landlord of the pub? But how could he kill someone that he'd chatted to over a drink, most nights? Bob used to say Matt was a smashing bloke, kind and generous. He'd give someone who was down on his luck a pint on the house. I can't believe Matt is a killer. Everybody likes Matt.'

* * *

'*Habeas corpus*,' announced Jack, apropos to nothing. 'Or more to the point, *infernum ubi corpus*?'

'Pardon?' Corrie poured him a small glass of the Old Tawny to go with his Stilton. She had no facts to support her suspicions, but she was convinced he'd develop gout if he drank too much of it. Added to which, he'd just put away a large plateful of liver and bacon. Carlene had given her a lecture about organ meats and their reputation as 'trigger purines'. Sometimes, Corrie thought that the more you knew about good nutrition, the less you enjoyed your food.

'Produce the body,' said Jack. 'It's a legal term. That's what I'm required to do.'

'What does the second bit mean?'

'Where the hell is the body?'

She laughed.

'I'm serious. Jolyon Richington-Blythe has to be somewhere close and I'm pretty certain he's dead. One minute, we're all sitting in the events suite waiting for his presentation. Then nobody can find him. That was days ago. The people that I believe are responsible for murdering him were taken into custody shortly after he disappeared. They didn't have time to dispose of the body anywhere complicated. So where is he?'

'Well, if you reckon Jolyon is still somewhere close by, I'm amazed nobody's tripped over his body.'

Jack put down his cheese knife and stared into the distance. It was a eureka moment. 'What did you just say?'

'I said I'm surprised no one has tripped over his body, if it's still lying around,' said Corrie. 'Metaphorically speaking, of course.'

'No, you didn't,' said Jack, capering around the kitchen. 'You said you were *amazed*.'

'Did I? OK, if you say so. What's the difference?'

'There's a huge difference. Because now I think I know where Jolyon's body is. It's in the bloody maze! Corrie, you're a genius.'

'I knew that. It's your turn to make the coffee.'

CHAPTER TWENTY-SEVEN

Jack called the whole team together for a briefing. Chief Superintendent Garwood lurked at the back, trying to look inconspicuous. Jack reckoned he'd come to make sure nobody proposed anything expensive.

'Brilliant work, everybody,' said Jack. 'We've arrested and charged two suspects for four murders and the attempted murder of Mrs Dawes, who, I am delighted to say, is fully recovered.' There were loud cheers. 'All that remains is to find the body — and I believe it to be a dead body — of Jolyon Richington-Blythe.'

'But, sir, we've searched everywhere,' complained someone at the back.

'Not quite everywhere.' Jack was wearing an expression that said, *I believe I've cracked this but I need your help.*

'Where d'you reckon he is, guv?' asked Bugsy.

'In the Richington Hall maze.'

It went quiet while they digested this. It was the one place they hadn't explored.

'I believe they kidnapped and killed him and didn't have much time to dispose of the body. It had to be somewhere close, but where it wouldn't be found until after they'd sabotaged the wine tanks and flown off to Bangkok.'

'You have to hand it to them,' said Mitch. 'That's bloody clever.'

'It might have been clever, if they hadn't been caught,' growled Garwood. 'They had a blasted nerve. Slaughtering their way through Richington Vale like a deadly Hansel and Gretel.'

'All they have left,' said Jack, 'is the small consolation of believing that we aren't going to find Jolyon's body.'

'But we are, aren't we sir?' said Aled. 'What will we do, send up a chopper?'

'Police helicopters are extremely expensive,' complained Garwood.

'No need for that, sir,' said Gemma. 'Why don't we just go in there and look for him? I've been round Hampton Court Maze. This one can't be much different. Then, if he isn't in there, we won't have wasted any public money.'

'Are you sure you know how to get in and out?' asked Aled. Gemma could talk a good fight but she wasn't always clear on the detail.

'Course. There's a technique for escaping from mazes. It's very simple, really. It's called "wall-following". You put one hand on the wall of the maze, it doesn't matter which one as long as you're consistent, then you keep walking, maintaining contact between your hand and the wall. Eventually, you either get to the centre, or you adopt the same procedure to get out.'

'That only works,' said Mitch, 'if it's a simple maze. If it's got sneaky short cuts via bridges or passage loops, you keep going round in circles. Do we know what kind of maze this is?'

'What we need is Trémaux's algorithm,' insisted Clive. 'It works in all cases, whatever the maze. Basically, if you reach a junction that you haven't previously seen, then you randomly select a way to go. If that takes you to a junction where one path's new, but the other isn't, then you select the new one. If you're choosing between a once or twice-used path, choose the one you used once, but never, ever, select a path that you've used twice. This method is guaranteed, eventually, to get you out of any maze. But it could take a long time.'

'Bloody hell, Clive, the maze will be full of very old coppers by the time we find Richington-Blythe.'

'I've got an idea,' declared Aled. 'Why don't we deploy a police camera drone? That way, we could see if the deceased is in there, without actually going in ourselves. Drone usage has proven rather handy to law enforcement lately, hasn't it? They reckon it will skyrocket over the next few years — no pun intended.'

'If he is in there,' said Garwood, 'the body will have to be airlifted out. There's no way a police vehicle will get between those narrow hedges and round all those tight bends. I'll need to discuss it with Sir Barnaby.' He marched to the door, then turned back. 'Well, what are you waiting for? Get on with it, Dawes.'

* * *

The police drone pilot was extremely skilful. They watched, fascinated, as she had a unique bird's-eye view in what was a time-critical search. Even better, she was able to livestream from the drone's video camera to several devices at once, which meant other officers didn't have to crowd around her to get a glimpse of her screen, or even worse, wait until the drone footage was downloaded. They were able to see what the drone could see, in real time.

After several passes over the maze, the drone hovered over the centre.

'Hold it there, please, and come down slightly, if possible,' said Jack.

And there it was — the body of Jolyon Richington-Blythe, as Jack's hunch had predicted. The corpse was slumped on the rustic bench and the crows had, indeed, feasted on the exposed parts.

'Maze or no maze, that is a crime scene,' decreed Garwood. Conscious that Jolyon had been perceived as an influential man by the community, Garwood knew this had to be done by the book if he was not to face criticism from several quarters, not least Sir Barnaby. 'We need a full SOCO team to determine time and cause of death and . . . er . . . any other information they may require, according to approved procedure. Carry on, Inspector.' He strode smartly back to his car, before somebody asked him how they were supposed to do it.

Back at the station, the discussion was, indeed, about how to get Dr Hardacre, her team and equipment to the crime scene, without vehicles and without having them wandering about, getting lost. They decided it wasn't practical to have continuous drone guidance for the number of journeys the procedure would require.

Clive's geek brain solved the problem. 'I've constructed a map, sir, from the drone video. It pinpoints the crime scene, with arrows to show the shortest way in and out. It can be loaded onto the devices of everyone who needs it. Satnav should do the rest. Any kit Doctor Hardacre considers essential can be wheeled in on a platform trolley.'

When they told her, Big Ron flatly refused. 'I'm not spending my valuable time fannying about in an overgrown shrubbery, pushing Marigold on a trolley. You can lower us in by helicopter. Sod the expense. When we've finished, you can winch us back out and airlift the body to the mortuary for the post-mortem. Do I make myself clear, Inspector?'

'Perfectly, Doctor.' And it was arranged thus.

Watching Big Ron and then Marigold Catwater dangling from a chopper was a sight Bugsy reckoned he would be unlikely to forget. Mercifully, they were both wearing protective suits, obscuring the onlookers' view of anything unseemly.

* * *

Both Jack and Bugsy attended the post-mortem. This was the last murder in the Bakers' killing spree, and the cause of death was a surprise.

'He had a massive cardiac arrest,' announced Dr Hardacre.

'Is that all?' asked Bugsy.

'You sound disappointed, Sergeant.'

'Only because this was supposed to be the big one,' added Jack. 'The star turn, to which all the other killings have been supporting acts.'

'We were expecting something a bit more spectacular than natural causes, I guess,' agreed Bugsy.

'Hold your horses, Sergeant. I haven't said he staggered into the maze and simply dropped dead from the effort. For a start, there's blunt force trauma to the back of his head. Possibly made by the concave end of a wine bottle, given the business he was in. But it wasn't enough to kill him. I examined the state of his clothes. He was in evening dress and wearing black patent shoes, which are badly scuffed at the heels. That indicates that he had been dragged for some distance. And look at this—' she pulled back the covering sheet — 'As you can see, the wildlife have made a meal of him, but these marks on his wrists and ankles reveal that, at some point, he had been tied to the wooden bench on which we found him. The SOCOs found the ropes that were used. They'd been discarded in another part of the maze. But this is what will really help you.'

She held up an evidence bag containing a vine-pruning knife. 'This was on the ground, under the bench. It's pretty old, but the blade is razor sharp. If you want me to speculate, Inspector, I'd say someone dragged him, unconscious, into the maze — someone who knew the shortcuts — tied him to the bench, then threatened him with the knife. He died of fright.'

'Please tell me they weren't wearing gloves,' begged Jack.

She smiled. 'It's your birthday, Inspector. There are two clear prints on the handle — thumb and forefinger.'

* * *

Nobody was surprised when the prints turned out to belong to Michael Baker. After he and his sister had been taken away on remand, the CPS added an additional charge of murder, in respect of Jolyon Richington-Blythe. Although, technically, he had died of a cardiac arrest, it was decided that it was brought on by the threatening behaviour of the prisoners, who intended to kill him and would have gone on to do so, if he hadn't already expired.

'Good work, team,' said Jack. It was the usual wash-up that Jack held at the end of a big investigation. This had been an especially gruelling one, but they'd reached a satisfactory conclusion with two people on remand awaiting trial for five murders, and both realistically facing life in prison. Mitch had been relieved when it was decided that he had been in no way responsible for Sandra's death.

'What a family,' said Bugsy.

'What do you think Sébastien and Marianne will do, now that there are only the two of them left?' wondered Gemma.

'Richington Vale Winery is no longer a viable business,' said Aled. 'They've lost most of the vines and all of last year's vintage. All they've got, really, is Richington Hall and the surrounding land.'

'But don't they own most of the village?' asked Gemma. 'All those shops and houses must be worth something.'

Bugsy shrugged. 'Would you want to go on living there, given what's happened? If I were Sébastien, I'd pack it in and go abroad.'

* * *

Sébastien and Marianne were in the offices of Leggett, Leggett & Fallover, where Peter Leggett was reading Jolyon's will.

'I'm very sorry for your loss. It has been a very traumatic time for you both.' He went on to explain that Jolyon had left them everything on the estate, jointly, including the workers' cottages, the shops in the village and the Blythe Spirit.

'Nothing to Zack?' asked Marianne.

'No, I'm afraid not. I had been in the process of drawing up divorce documents for Sandra, which included provision for their son, when she sadly passed.' He looked sombre. 'I have to tell you that the financial health of Richington Vale Winery is not good. Your father made a lot of unwise investments, and borrowed an awful lot in order to keep the vineyard going. He mortgaged all the properties he owned very heavily, including Richington Hall. The bank had been on the point of foreclosing when he died. Now they will want everything that's left.'

Sébastien and Marianne looked at each other in dismay.

'So what you're telling us is that all we have inherited is a great deal of debt,' said Sébastien.

'Seb, whatever shall we do?' Marianne was tearful. 'We shan't even have a roof over our heads now.'

Sébastien was angry. He got up and began to pace about. 'What in the world was Father thinking? When I proposed a takeover by that Californian wine company, it was a multi-million-dollar deal. They'd agreed to keep on all our workers and offered opportunities in the United States, too. It was a once-in-a-lifetime offer. Why the hell did he turn it down?'

'You know why,' said Marianne. 'He was fanatical about preserving Grandfather's legacy — his precious memory.'

Sébastien snorted. 'What's the point of worshipping the dead at the expense of the living? Father was a fool.'

'Yes, and in the end, it got him killed.'

Peter Leggett coughed. 'That brings me to the last item we need to discuss. Your father made me swear never to disclose this, but now he's dead, the information belongs to his next of kin.'

They looked at the lawyer. 'Spit it out, man,' ordered Seb.

'The land that the house and vineyard occupy, and more importantly, the extra land your father bought in 1989 to expand the business, is prime building land. He didn't want you to know, because he was sure you would want to sell the vineyard for development.'

Leggett shuffled his papers, while he waited for this to sink in. 'I have discussed this, hypothetically, with the chief planning officer,' he continued, 'and he is of the opinion that planning permission would be viewed favourably. The village of Richington Vale has grown considerably over the years and now there is a need for more affordable houses, a bigger school, supermarkets, and many more amenities that a town, rather than a village, would expect to enjoy. Given the circumstances, my advice would be to sell to the highest bidder.'

Sébastien resisted the urge to cheer, as it would appear unseemly so soon after his father's death. 'That's exactly what we'll do. Agreed, Marianne?'

'What about our workers? Some of them have been with us all their working lives.' Marianne was concerned.

'There'll be work and houses for them in Richington Newtown.' Sébastien was thinking way ahead. 'And they'll get paid proper wages and work in decent conditions.'

'Yes, I see. It can only be good for everybody.'

'And a much better memorial to the old air commodore than a failing vineyard with a reputation for malpractice and grisly murder.'

CHAPTER TWENTY-EIGHT

They made their way towards the hole in the fence, and immediately, childhood memories flooded back. They climbed through, and there it stood, dark and hulking. The dilapidated sign, now hanging lopsided off a single hook, declared the derelict building was once Richington Vale Children's Home. The path to the door was littered with broken glass, cans and fast-food containers, thrown there by the teenagers of the village, who came here to hang out.

Miles shuddered. He stared at the haunted building. It stared back at him, daring him not to be afraid.

'Do we have to go inside, Sheila? Can't we just do what we came to do, then go home?'

'You know we can't. We have to make absolutely sure that there's nobody inside. Trust me. It will help us to move on if we confront our demons before we destroy them.'

They walked towards the door. Miles thought the sinking feelings of misery and fear would cease when he went inside. They didn't. He thought it would feel smaller than he remembered. It didn't. The whole structure felt monstrous and massive. It looked as big as it ever had. Then he glimpsed a patch of sky through a hole in the roof, as if it were a message, telling him that it was all over. But it wasn't. Not yet.

Inside, Sheila paused outside a splintered door, sagging off its hinges. It led down to the cellar. Once, there had been a bolt on the outside, but it had long since rusted away. She recalled the many times she had been locked away down there and left for many hours, sometimes overnight, or for a whole day. It happened mostly when she had tried to protect her little brother from a beating. He had wet the bed from sheer terror on many occasions and been made to sleep in it, cold and stinking. She had defended him bravely, despite the awful consequences.

'Do you remember how the food improved and we had heating on the days the council inspectors called?' asked Sheila.

'And when we went to school, Miss Chambers used to share her lunch with us, because we were always hungry.'

Miles picked up a broken flowerpot from among the debris on the floor. 'I remember this pot. Miss Chambers gave us all a sunflower seed and I planted mine in this. I must have been about seven. I tended it every day until it grew a flower, bright and yellow, like the sun. I was so proud of it. Then, when we were allowed to take our plants home, I took it to show Miss Shrike, thinking she'd be pleased with me.'

'Instead,' said Sheila, 'she pulled it out of the pot and threw it on the fire. You cried all night.'

'Why did she do that? What was so wrong with growing a flower, that I had to be punished?' Miles remembered his wretchedness, as if it had only just happened.

'She didn't destroy it because it was wrong,' said Sheila. 'She did it because the sunflower made you happy. It was just another way to hurt you. She was a despicable, cruel, vindictive human being. She deserved to suffer, and I have no regrets about what happened to her.'

'It was sad what happened to Miss Chambers, though. She never did recognize us, after we came back, bless her. I guess we have changed a lot over the years.'

Sheila nodded. 'It could be that she confused us with another brother and sister with auburn hair. I'm glad they caught the woman who poisoned her. There's such evil in some people.'

One of the rooms had been badly damaged by fire. Sheila pushed open what remained of the blackened door. 'Here's Miss Shrike's sitting room. None of us children dared come in here, on pain of punishment. It was the only room that was heated in winter. Do you remember, Miles, how she used to sit in front of her log fire in that awful old flannel nightdress, drinking cocoa laced with whisky. She'd fall asleep, warm and cosy, while we all froze in our beds.'

Miles was silent for a while. 'Sheila, do you remember our mother?'

'Not really. I was only three when she left. You were just a baby.'

'Why do you suppose she left us?'

'Miss Shrike said she'd gone abroad with her new boyfriend and didn't want us anymore. We were a nuisance. And now she had the bother of looking after us. She said we should never have been born.'

'Do you think that was true?'

'It might have been. But don't let's think about that. It was a long time ago and our lives are happy now. We just need to put an end to the nightmares, once and for all.'

Miles turned to go back outside, where they'd parked the car by the roadside. 'I'll fetch the petrol.'

Satisfied that there was no one in the house, and being on the rural outskirts of the village, that nobody could be affected by what they were doing, Miles carefully filled a Richington Vale magnum bottle with petrol and stuffed a rag in the neck. They stood as far back as they could, but just close enough to stay within range. He took out a box of matches.

'Shall I do it now, Sheila?'

'Yes, Miles. Be careful.'

He lit the rag, then quickly hurled the bottle with all his strength through an upstairs window. They heard it land. A split second later, the building burst into spectacular flames, crackling, sputtering and popping — a roaring blaze that quickly spread via the combustible rubbish in all the rooms. Doors and window frames creaked and snapped before tumbling into ashes.

They watched it burn for a while. Fire was destroying their nemesis, but it was also purifying it, with the generative power of new life, energy and change. For Sheila and Miles, the flames represented illumination, enlightenment and — most of all — karma.

'It's in such a bad state, it'll be just a blackened shell by the time anyone sees the fire. Too far gone to save it, that's if anyone even bothers to try.' Miles was feeling better than he had for years.

Sheila took one last look. 'All this time, there's only one passage from the Bible that has given us the strength to carry on, to come back and do this.'

Miles nodded. '*Our God is a consuming fire.* Hebrews 12:29.' He smiled. 'Sorry, Reverend.'

They walked back to the road and drove home to make cocoa, laced with whisky.

* * *

'Seems the old children's home has burned down — what was left of it.' Sergeant Parsloe had come up to the MIT room, ostensibly to share the fact, but, in reality, to cadge a cup of coffee and a chocolate digestive. 'The vicar isn't at all happy. Bang goes his boxing club. Mind you, it isn't the first time there's been a fire in that place.'

'What happened, Norman?' asked Bugsy. 'Was it an accident?'

'Dunno about this time, but they didn't reckon the last fire was an accident. They were pretty certain it was started by one of the kiddies, but they could never prove anything. Poor little buggers had a miserable enough existence as it was. I was only a young constable back then, but the stories you heard made your hair curl.' He ran a hand over his bald head. 'Course, I had hair, back then.'

'Why didn't somebody do something about it?' asked Gemma. She firmly believed that the world would be a better place if more people took action against injustice when they came across it, instead of turning a blind eye.

'Because whenever the council visited, everything looked fine. When they questioned the children, they said they were happy, no complaints and they were well looked after. They felt lucky to be there, after being dumped by their parents. After the fire, when the council closed it down, the truth came out. They'd had to say what the woman in charge told them, or they'd have got a beating, or been starved for twenty-four hours.'

'That's terrible,' said Gemma. 'Who was she? Is she still around?'

'Her name was Hilda Shrike,' said Clive, tapping away. 'I've found the news item on the *Richington Echo* archive website. Apparently, it was her habit, on a cold winter night, to sit in front of the open log fire in her private room and enjoy a cup of cocoa before going to bed. On this particular January evening, a burning log fell from the fire and set her nightgown alight. She was burned alive.'

'How come she didn't wake up and run outside?' asked Aled. 'Someone might have been able to put out the flames.'

'The post-mortem found whisky in her system, which would have made her groggy, I guess. The question they asked at the time was, why had she removed the fireguard? She always put it in front of the fire, to stop cinders falling out and burning holes in her rug. After the fire service had put out the fire, they found that it had been moved to one side and the fire tongs were lying in the grate.'

Clive scrolled down the site further. 'For a while, there was a suspicion that one of the children might have deliberately moved the guard, and used the tongs to pull out a burning log and ignite Miss Shrike's nightie. That's probably just lurid *Echo* speculation, to drive up circulation.' He read on. 'It says all the children were safely evacuated, and the council, whose responsibility it had been to finance and maintain the home, decided that under the tragic circumstances, it should be left empty until it could be sold. Since no one was interested in buying it, it became derelict. The kids were moved elsewhere, apart from one or two who were old enough to leave and live independently. No further action was taken.'

'Do we know how the building caught fire this time, Norman?' asked Bugsy.

'Youngsters mucking around and setting fire to rubbish with petrol, the fire service reckons. They're always at it. Bloody dangerous. We questioned some of the likely lads that hang around, but they all claimed they weren't there when it started. There was a rave in someone's garage and they were all there. We checked it out.'

'Is there going to be any further investigation?' asked Aled.

'Doubt it. Not much point. The building was derelict anyway and nobody was hurt. It belonged to the council, who were going to allow a change of use, so the vicar could set up a boxing club. He'll have to find somewhere else now.'

CHAPTER TWENTY-NINE

'Jack, do you remember me telling you that when I was looking out of the window at the winery, I could see the dead vines? They were in a particular shape, and I've just remembered what it was.'

Jack was about to sink his teeth into one of Corrie's homemade pasties. He'd poured himself a beer and there was rugby on the television. He wasn't sure that the shape of dead vines was his top priority. 'Surprise me.'

'Well, it was strange at the time, but it isn't now we know it was Matt poisoning them. I mean, Michael Baker. I'm still having trouble getting my head around Matt Brown being a murderer. I could understand it being the Wine Woman — she was a shifty piece of work. *Nobody* is ever that slim and clever and attractive and vivacious, all at the same time. You could tell she was false, and I'm not biased because she tried to drown me. But Matt? Everyone liked Matt.'

'Corrie, my beer's getting warm. What was the shape?'
'T.'

'No thanks, I've got a beer. What was the shape?'

'I just told you. It was T-shaped. There was a wide band of brown across the top of the vineyard and another one down the middle. It was a big letter T.'

Jack looked blank. 'Should that mean something?'

'Honestly, Jack, for a detective you're pretty slow on the uptake. It was T for Thomas — his father's name. It was his way of saying, "I'm doing this for you, Dad."'

'Very touching. If that was all he'd done, I might have some sympathy, but between them they killed five people, two of whom played no part in his father's death or his mother's poverty, or the fact that both he and his sister went off the rails. People have choices. Can I watch the rugby now, please? There's another big match on Saturday night, but I need to watch this one first. It doesn't work if you don't see them in sequence.'

'Aah,' said Corrie. 'You'll have to record the Saturday one.'

'Why? If I record it, I'm bound to know the result before I watch it. Some smart-arse always lets it slip.'

'We're going out on Saturday night. Antoine's parents are having a house-warming party.'

'I didn't know they'd moved,' said Jack. 'Didn't they have that big town house in Kings Richington, so they'd be near all their London restaurants?'

'They still have. But now they have a big country manor in Richington Vale as well. They've bought Richington Hall in a repossession deal. Carlene says it was mortgaged up to the eyeballs, so it was a snip.'

'Are they taking over the vineyard and winery, too?'

'No. According to Mrs Bloxham, who cleans for Mrs Cheadle, who's the daughter-in-law of the chief planning officer's gardener, there isn't going to be a vineyard for much longer. The land has been sold for development. They're going to grow houses on it instead of vines, and a jolly good job, I say. I'll find out how much they paid for it from Peter Leggett, when we get chatting over the buffet.'

Jack grinned. 'I reckon you fancy him. I haven't forgotten the time you cooked him a hog roast and let him have the stuffing for free.'

'Excuse me. I'm basically a very cerebral and creative person. I don't go around panting for bodily contact over the canapés, like a confused corgi.'

'Don't tell me you're going to do the catering for this party,' said Jack.

'No, I'm blooming well not! Monsieur and Madame Dubois, that's Antoine's mum and dad, are bringing in their own chef from Le Canard Bleu, so I get to have a Saturday night off and enjoy the party. Everyone's going, including George and Cynthia, Bugsy and Iris, even Sir Barnaby and Lady Lobelia, so we get to catch up on all the goss.'

'Oh good. Is there anyone else I need to avoid?'

Corrie rolled her eyes. 'Sébastien and Marianne are coming to say goodbye. Now they've sold the house and the land, they're off to California to work for a Napa Valley wine company. Let's hope this time around, they can find partners who don't poison people or end up knifed in the chest, although I guess you never know with California, if the television dramas are to be believed. I'll have to try on my posh frock and you can wear your dinner suit, if you can still do up the trousers. Won't it be fun?'

'Riveting,' said Jack. 'I can hardly wait.'

* * *

Antoine's parents had obviously been impressed by the strong French influence of the décor, because they'd hardly changed a thing. The Louis XVI drawing room still displayed the heavy brocade curtains and matching upholstery, and the pair of art deco cameo glass vases held extravagant bunches of professionally arranged flowers, obviously the work of Sheila and Miles Barton, as a house-warming present.

Sébastien and Marianne had tried hard to put the terrible events of the last months behind them and were looking forward to a new future in a new country. They chatted to Monsieur and Madame Dubois in French, and Marianne even managed the occasional weak smile. They were not sorry to be leaving their childhood home. Since the death of their mother, nothing had felt right. When Jolyon married Sandra, life had gone from bad to worse. But they didn't regard Zack with any malice. If anything, he had been a victim, too.

Bugsy, uncomfortable in a fancy evening shirt with a tight collar and bow tie, was admiring a painting, hanging in a recess. 'Look, Iris, it's a pond with waterlilies.'

'It's a Monet,' said Iris. 'He painted lots of them.'

'Looks like he did this one in the rain, the paint's gone all runny.'

Iris scolded him. 'It's supposed to be like that. He was an Impressionist. And he had cataracts.' She shoved him. 'Don't lean against the alcove — you'll sweat on the wallpaper. Isn't this a beautiful room, Mike? Wouldn't you like to live in a house like this?'

He kissed her on the cheek. 'I'd be happy living anywhere, as long as it was with you, my love. I'm going over to the buffet table to get some food. Those lobster tarts aren't going to eat themselves.'

While he was reaching for a plate, he noticed Sheila Barton helping herself to some salad. As she picked up the server, her sleeve fell back and revealed a scar on her arm. It looked like an old burn. She noticed his glance and pulled her sleeve over it, hastily.

'That looks like it was nasty, love. How did it happen?'

'I had an accident as a child — got too close to the fire.' She smiled and moved away, remembering how the tongs had slipped out of her hand when she pulled the burning log from the fire and placed it against Miss Shrike's nightdress. The flames had flared up faster than she'd expected and singed her arm. But that was all in the past now. She went to find Miles, to give him his plate of food.

Carlene came to find Corrie and Cynthia, who were sampling the wine.

'Are you enjoying yourself, Mrs D?'

'Well, it's nice not to be head cook and carrot-scrubber for a change,' said Corrie, pouring herself a generous glass of Sauvignon Blanc.

'I see that nearly drowning in it hasn't put you ladies off the wine.' Jack, still affected by the incident, had wandered over to find Corrie. 'What a terrible waste. All those gallons of Chardonnay down the drain. Pity we couldn't have rescued some of it.'

'Trust me, you wouldn't have wanted to drink it, even if we had,' said Corrie.

'Why?'

'Because while I was drowning and fighting for breath, I peed in it.'

'So did I,' added Carlene.

'Me too,' giggled Cynthia.

EPILOGUE

'Three sets of brothers and sisters,' mused Corrie. She was sitting with her feet up for a change, and having time to think made her philosophical. 'Such different outcomes for each of them.'

'Like what?' asked Jack. He was more of an action man than a philosopher — it went with the job.

'Take Sébastien and Marianne. They each had hopes of a life with a soulmate. Instead, they're emigrating to lead new single lives. I hope they each find what they're looking for.'

Jack put down his copy of the *Echo*. 'I'm not sure they know what that is yet. They're still a bit shocked — like rabbits in headlights. It isn't every day that your father, step-mother and partner all die, one after the other.'

Corrie couldn't even imagine what that would feel like. 'Then there's Suzy and Matt — I mean, Samantha and Michael. They've been sentenced to life, and the judge recommended that they serve at least thirty years. They'll be pensioners when they come out.'

'It's a warning that you can't go around bumping people off, no matter how justified you believe you are. Who are the third brother and sister?' Jack wondered.

Corrie toyed with the stem of her wine glass, thoughtfully. 'Sheila and Miles Barton. There's a backstory there, but no one seems to know what it is. They have seemed a lot happier of late, so that's good, and they've certainly had a lot of demand for funeral flowers, now that the police have released the bodies. They're fundraising like mad to help the vicar collect enough money to start a boxing gym. He wants a purpose-built one on the new estate.' She reflected for a moment. 'It was a shame about the vineyard. The views over the vines were wonderfully uplifting. But I can see that the village was bursting at the seams. It's a good opportunity for everyone.'

* * *

It was a time for renewal in Richington Vale. Old billboards were coming down and new ones were going up. The elaborate sign on the outskirts of the village welcoming visitors to *Richington Vale Winery, the home of award-winning wines,* had been taken down and burned. Instead, a new board proclaimed, *Welcome to Richington Newtown. Please Drive Carefully.*

The road through the village still followed the River Richington as it chortled its way down to the Thames, and the ducks and swans still swam on the water meadow. Old-fashioned shops still lined the narrow streets, but now there were road signs pointing to where retail parks, industrial estates and a brand new Richington Academy would soon spring up.

The sign outside the Blythe Spirit had also been removed. Now there was a colourful board depicting an eagle-like bird, wings spread and flying up out of the flames and ashes of a fire. The pub was now called the Phoenix Rising.

The name of the licensee over the door was Zack Richington. Zack had dropped the hyphenated Blythe, which he said had bad vibes for him. Sébastien and Marianne had shared the proceeds from the sale of the vineyard with their half-brother. He had bought the pub and now ran it with his wife, Rosie Richington. She joked that saying her married name was like chewing a toffee, but it pleased her father.

Freddy remained in the kitchen, turning out his famous hotpots, sad but resigned. He never visited Mikey.

* * *

'Georgie, come and look at this.' Cynthia held up a copy of the *Echo*. 'Here's another one for your scrapbook.'

George Garwood pottered in from the herbaceous borders, wearing his gardening jacket. 'Cynthia, I keep telling you. It isn't a scrapbook, it's a . . .' He peered over her shoulder. 'I say, that's rather a good one of me, isn't it?'

The *Echo* photographer had taken a shot of Garwood with the chief planning officer and the construction manager, all wearing hard hats and standing on a pile of rubble. Around them were excavators, bulldozers and cranes, with teams of labourers who had once pruned vines and made wine. The caption read, *Birth of a New Development. Richington Newtown goes urban.*

The pile of rubble had once been a monument. In among the shattered, honey-coloured stone, there was a brass plaque. If you looked closely at the photograph, you could just make out the inscription.

This vineyard was founded by Air Commodore Sir Donald Richington-Blythe DFC. 1919–1989.

THE END

ALSO BY FRANCES LLOYD

DETECTIVE INSPECTOR JACK DAWES
MYSTERY SERIES

Thank you for reading this book.

If you enjoyed it please leave feedback on Amazon or Goodreads, and if there is anything we missed or you have a question about, then please get in touch. We appreciate you choosing our book.

Founded in 2014 in Shoreditch, London, we at Joffe Books pride ourselves on our history of innovative publishing. We were thrilled to be shortlisted for Independent Publisher of the Year at the British Book Awards.

www.joffebooks.com

We're very grateful to eagle-eyed readers who take the time to contact us. Please send any errors you find to corrections@joffebooks.com. We'll get them fixed ASAP.